# THE BOY UPSTAIRS

AMANDA SHELLEY

Visit my website at
www.amandashelley.com

# CONNECT WITH AMANDA SHELLEY

Want to be the first to know about upcoming sales and new releases? Make sure you sign up for my newsletter as well as connect with me on social media and your favorite retail store.

Website:
www.amandashelley.com
Newsletter:
https://geni.us/AmandaShelleyNL
Facebook:
https://www.facebook.com/authoramandashelley/
Instagram:
https://www.instagram.com/authoramandashelley/
Reader's Group:
https://www.facebook.com/groups/AmandasArmyofReaders/
Tik Tok:
https://www.tiktok.com/@authoramandashelley
Amazon:
https://www.amazon.com/author/amandashelley
Goodreads:

https://www.goodreads.com/author/show/19713563.Aman
da_Shelley
Book Bub:
https://www.bookbub.com/profile/amanda-shelley

## ABOUT THE BOOK

**The Boy Upstairs**

**I ran into Derek while trying to escape the neighbor from hell.**

Instantly, we hit it off. Since he's only here for three months and the microbrewery leaves me little time for commitments, it's the perfect setup for a fling.

He's adventurous, challenges me, and he just gets me from the inside out.

With our expiration date quickly approaching, I'm left to wonder... *Will my heart ever be the same without the boy upstairs?*

# Chapter 1
## Derek

BANG. Bang. Bang.

A muffled "Oh, yes," comes through the thin walls of my new apartment. "Right there..."

A loud growl comes from a man as he gives it his all. "Fuck yeah, beautiful..."

Bang... Bang...

I swear if he gives it to her any harder, they'll join me in bed.

I'm not a prude, but I'm not interested in the company either.

Jesus. Fucking. Christ.

*Haven't they heard of putting a pillow between the wall and the headboard?*

I haven't met my neighbors since moving in last week, but they're leaving one hell of an impression. They've been going at it all night like rabbits, and this is beyond ridiculous.

One perk of having this new client is that he's letting me stay here for one hell of a deal, but waking up at the ass-crack of dawn to someone's sexcapades may be more than I bargained for.

Bang. Squeak. Bang.

"Ahhhh... So close..." she moans again, completely in the

throes of passion. It's like a bad porno scene is playing out beside me, and I can't fucking get away from it. Not only do I get to hear the thumping, but she's a talker and loves giving the play-by-play.

"For the love of Pete, finish already," I grumble to myself as I flip my pillow and cover my ears with my other pillow.

"Hold on... beautiful," he grunts in return.

"No... don't hold on." Why can't you be a three-pump chump?

Hell, I'm all for getting lost in a woman. Trust me, but this Pete fella is working my last nerve. If I hear about how big his cock is one more time, I'm gonna scream, "Then show her how you fucking use it. Get the job done, man."

"So big..."

We all get it, lady. The man's got a magic Johnson.

There are some things I just never need to know, especially about my neighbors.

Tossing over, I glance at the clock. It's almost six. There has to be a café open by now where I can grab some coffee and get a break from the fuck bunnies. I have a big project and a tight deadline. I can't afford to be dead on my feet.

"Oh God... Oh God... Oh God."

"That's it," I grumble, tossing back the covers and clamber out of bed. "I'm outta here."

Needing to make a quick escape, I pull on my jeans from yesterday and grab a clean shirt before making my way to the bathroom. Normally, I'm the type who won't fully wake up without a shower, but thanks to my nympho neighbors, I'm high tailing it out of here like my ass is on fire.

Fuck, I miss my house, I miss my privacy, and most important, I miss the fact that I never heard my neighbors.

Stopping at the bathroom, I realize I've made the right choice. Even through a closed door, there's no escaping her fucking screams. After splashing some water on my face and slapping on some deodorant, I run my fingers through my hair to tame my bed head.

They're still going hot and heavy when I get to the kitchen, grab my keys, and bolt out the door. Hell, I can still hear banging when I get outside my four-plex and make my way to the stairs.

Did she slip the dude a little blue pill or something?

The man's a fuckin' machine.

When I reach the bottom, a door opens and out steps the sexy woman I met the day I moved in. A dark hoodie covers the half-sleeve tattoo that drew my attention to her earlier.

When her electric-blue eyes dance, she smiles. "Mornin', Derek. Fancy meeting you here. Couldn't sleep?"

Rolling my eyes in the offenders' direction, I mumble, "Uh, yeah... that's an understatement."

Tessa adorably covers her mouth to hold back a laugh as she quickly adds, "You'd think Pete was hung like a God, by the way she's goin' on about him. For the love of fuck... get 'er done, dude."

"No kidding," I agree. "I'm all for going at it all night long... but usually I'm not banging on my neighbor's walls either."

"Ouch... that must've been rough. It was bad enough downstairs."

"No kidding." But I've given the nymphs too much of my time already and would rather turn my attention to her. "Where are you heading off to?"

"Anywhere but here." She smirks adorably, and I grin.

"Is there a place in town to get some decent coffee?"

"Oh... coffee sounds so good right now. I didn't get home until after three, and I could use a cup about now if I have to survive today."

Whoa. Late night. But instead of prying, I suggest, "You're welcome to join me. I'll drive if you navigate."

Her dark lashes blink a few times as if she's hesitating.

"Or you can drive yourself if you'd rather fly solo." I offer as an out.

"No..." she spits out. "Sorry, I... uh, would love to join you. Obviously, I need a caffeine drip for an IV if I can't even answer your simple question. Steaming Cups has the best coffee in town. There's also a breakfast sandwich that's to die for. I hope you're hungry."

With each of us having designated parking spots, I point to my trusty Land Rover and click the button to unlock it. It was my first new-to-me purchase after college and has done me well over the years. I wouldn't think of trading it in anytime soon.

"So you're from Washington?" Tessa asks once we get out of the parking lot.

"Uh, yeah?" How does she know?

I see from the corner of my eyes Tessa shake her head. "Make a right at the next block. Your plates gave you away."

Ah. Makes sense.

"What brought you to Bear Creek?"

"My latest client needs me here to help him with branding as he gets everything ready for his presentation to his angel investor."

"Must be a pretty big client if you're willing to relocate."

"Oh, this isn't permanent. I'll head back to Seattle in October."

"Make a left, then go two blocks. Steaming Cups is on the next block. Just park out front on the street. Do you relocate for all your clients?"

"No, this is a first," I admit as I pull into a parking space.

"Sounds like there's a story."

Shrugging, I admit, "Not really. I've been a freelance graphic designer for some time now, while working full time for an advertising company. As of this week, I'm officially on my own. What's funny is when I put in my notice, they agreed to pay me more to keep me on as a consultant than when I was on salary."

"That must be nice," Tessa says as she opens the door and hops out before I have the chance to move from my seat. "I like being my own boss, too."

Once we're out of the vehicle, I ask, "What is it that you do?"

Her smile widens when she announces, "I'm the proud owner of Bed Knobs & Brews, a local microbrewery here in town."

"Bed Knobs?" Interesting choice for branding.

"The storefront is three blocks over just off Main Street. The site used to be an old B&B, so I played on words to remind people where it's located. Being in a tourist town, you gotta stay creative to be remembered. All the booths in the restaurant look like old headboards."

Sounds like something right up my alley. "I'll have to check it out sometime. I love a good microbrew."

"Oh, we've got the best in town," Tessa praises.

Walking into the diner, a friendly older waitress greets us. "Mornin', Tessa. Who's this fella you've brought with you?"

"Mornin', Miss Mable. This is my neighbor Derek."

"What brings you all in so early? Normally, I see you in for the lunch rush."

Tessa sighs as we're shown to an open booth. "A noisy neighbor."

"Oh, those are the worst. I haven't lived in an apartment since I was your age, but I do remember how thin those walls could be," Miss Mable says as she punches her hip with her fist.

"Our walls are definitely too thin," I grumble under my breath.

Mable's brows shoot up to her graying hairline. "You'd call the cops if domestic violence was involved, right?"

Tessa looks to me, then tries to hold back a laugh. "Oh, I don't think anyone was being hurt, Miss Mable. From the sounds of it, the bed was rockin', and I wasn't about to go knockin'... If you know what I mean."

Did Tessa just say that? Mable's practically my mother's age. There's no way I'd talk about the sexcapade we heard in front of her.

"I suppose you're right. Everyone needs a little action now and then. Good for them."

As my jaw drops to the table, Tessa and Mable burst into laughter.

There goes my impression of sweet and innocent Miss Mable.

When Tessa regains control enough to talk, she demands, "Derek, don't be such a prude. That was some funny shit right there, and you know it."

The moment she smirks in my direction, I lose it, and the three of us fill the room with laughter.

Holy shit, I've gotta stay on my toes with this one.

Once we reclaim our composure, we put in an order for our caffeine fix in to-go cups. Tessa with a tall vanilla latte and myself with an extra-large americano. When Miss Mable returns, I follow Tessa's suggestion and order the breakfast sandwich special.

As soon as we're alone, Tessa asks, "So what do you think of Bear Creek so far?"

"Honestly, I've spent most of my time behind a computer screen or with clients," I admit, hoping that will change soon. Otherwise, what's the point of relocating?

"You've been here a week, right? That seems fair. What'd you do for fun in Seattle?"

"Hmmm... let's see... I spent a lot of my free time doing freelance work, but when I'd take a break, I'd hang with my friends or family in the city. We also hike, kayak, ride bikes along the trails, and fish when I visit my grandparents or sister on the island."

"Island?" Tessa asks with interest.

"My grandparents and now sister... I guess... have a place on Anderson Island. It's a small Island in Puget Sound, just south of Tacoma."

"Are you close to your family?"

"You could say that." I smile at the memory of Dani's latest surprise. I may be out a hundred bucks, but she was right—her plans were worth it.

Tessa cocks her head to the side as if she's studying my features. "What's so funny?"

Shaking off my thoughts, I chortle. "I lost a bet with my sister the last time we were together. She'd made us dress up—under the premise of family photos but threw in a surprise wedding. My brothers and I were shocked, but we had fun all the same—that's a hundred bucks I'm happy to part with."

"That would be shocking," Tessa agrees before Miss Mable interrupts to bring our food.

"Here ya go. If you need anything, you just holler."

"Thank you, Miss Mable. We will," Tessa assures her.

We take a moment to enjoy the mouthwatering breakfast sandwich. It's the perfect combination of eggs, bacon, pesto, and cheese. Just as I take another bite, Tessa reminds me, "You said brothers. Do you have a big family?"

Nodding, I finish chewing. "Yeah. I'm the oldest of four. Dani is next in line, then Damien, and Davis."

"Wow, your mom had her hands full."

"You'd think the biggest problem would be us boys, but Dani gave Mom a run for her money. She always had to out-do us and prove she could best us at anything she set her mind to.

That is, until she discovered books. Once she got lost in those, she, for the most part, left us alone—until she felt the need to be competitive. Then all bets were off."

"Oh my," Tessa says, placing a napkin over her face, holding back laughter.

"Mom. She was fine. It was us boys who were in for it. That girl may have been scrawny, but she sure was scrappy. Thank God, she's grown out of it for the most part." I laugh as I realize how she's still tenacious and won't let anything get in her way, but she's more refined in her approach.

"I'm an only child." Tessa lets out a sigh as she admits, "But being raised by my dad, I suppose I was scrappy, too. In first grade, I punched a boy for tugging on my ponytail, and no one bothered me since. Benefits of living in a small town, I guess."

"Dani would've done the same," I admit. Though she didn't need to punch anyone. Having three brothers, word got around quickly in our small town not to mess with her—though she's feisty enough, we never needed interventions.

But enough about Dani. I'm more interested in the woman across from me right now. "Have you lived in Bear Creek long?"

"I grew up outside of town, but other than attending the University of Colorado, yes." Her lips pull into a beautiful smile at the end, helping an unknown dimple make its appearance. For a moment, all I can do is stare.

This woman's natural beauty runs circles around the glamour magazine girls. From her dark pixie cut, to her long, thick lashes, she doesn't need a stitch of makeup. As I look closer, there's a light dusting of freckles across the bridge of her nose. Her most mesmerizing feature though, are her eyes. I've never seen a shade similar. There's a navy ring around a brighter, almost cobalt blue in the center, that has me staring longer—just to decipher the color.

God, I'm a graphic design artist, and I can't get it right. Thankfully, she doesn't notice and continues chatting about her life.

"When I started my business, I moved to town so I could be closer. Besides—even though my grandparents have passed, and Dad's still on the road a lot, at twenty-six, I'd rather not live at home... if ya know what I mean."

"Same. I haven't lived at home since summers in college. I love my family, but I was ready to be on my own, too. What does your dad do if he travels a lot?"

"Oh. He's a long-haul trucker. Has been his entire life. It's how he met my mom before I was born. She was from Phoenix and worked as a waitress. He kept going out of his way to see her often and eventually, they fell in love and got married. I came along about two years later, after she'd traveled with him for a bit..." Tessa's casual posture stiffens as she trails off.

Something's not right.

"Does she still travel with him?" I ask, hoping I'm not prying.

"Unfortunately, she died in childbirth with me," Tessa says with a matter-of-fact tone, making my stomach drop to my toes. I certainly didn't see that coming. Tessa must notice my reaction because she quickly adds, "Don't worry. I would've loved to have known my mom, but I've still had an amazing life. Dad brought me home to live with his parents, and my grandma helped me in every way she knew how."

I'm at a loss for words. She seems at peace with everything, but I don't want to say the wrong thing and come off sounding like a complete asshat.

"Sorry, I didn't mean to dump information on you." Tessa shrugs. "Living here my whole life, I forget people don't know."

My mom was the center of our universe as kids, I can't imagine never knowing her.

"No need to apologize. Does your dad get home often?"

"He's home about every other week. I check in on the place while he's gone, but since we live outside of town, and my employees from the brewery are there often, no one bothers the place much. The apartment's much closer to work and with my long hours, I'd rather not make a commute, too."

"Speaking of apartments... should I expect this thing with Pete to be a regular occurrence?" I cringe, wanting to forget about this morning, yet needing to be prepared.

A smile plays on her lips. "No. Thank God. That's actually Hannah's place. They just got engaged, and she'll be moving out to be with him at the end of the month. So only another week or two, tops."

Thank fuck. "That's a relief," comes out on a sigh. "Not sure how much more I could handle. I've never missed my house more than today. That's for sure."

"No kidding," Tessa practically snorts. "I was willing to drive twenty miles out of town, just to get some peace."

"At least you've got options," I tease. "I'm not keeping you from sleep, am I?"

Shaking her head, "No. I have a meeting at ten, then I'll be free for the day. Hopefully things will have settled down by the time we get back."

"I'm meeting a client this morning, too. Then if my apartment is quiet enough, I'll crank out a few other designs this afternoon."

"We've got a live band tonight, so I'll be back at work this evening. They usually start around eight. They're just starting out and play mostly covers, but they've got a few originals that might take them a lot further than Bed Knobs & Brews. But I'm the one who discovered them first and gave them their first shot."

"Ah... talent scout as well, eh?"

Rolling her eyes, Tessa grins. "It's nepotism actually. My best friend Nita and I were hanging out earlier this summer, and her brother was home from college, practicing in their garage with his band. They caught my ear, and I offered them a short-term gig for Thursdays throughout the summer. It was a win-win. I have live entertainment, and they get experience. With the USA Music Festival happening in Bear Creek this month, it'll give them exposure. You never know who will be in town looking for raw talent."

"That's true. Look at Ed Sheeran. He was discovered by Jamie Foxx at an open-mic night in LA."

Tessa's perfectly sculpted brow arches. "That's an extremely specific fact. A big Ed Sheeran fan, are you?"

"Actually, I am," I admit. The dude is fuckin' talented. "I

recently watched an interview that asked how he started. All I'm sayin' is—you never know who'll discover you when you're working your ass off for your dreams."

"Are you a musician, too?" Tessa asks with interest.

"Hell no. I can barely carry a tune in a bucket. But I know what it's like to work for something." Being here in Bear Creek is living proof of that. There's no way I would've picked up and moved across the country, if branching out on my own wasn't so important to me.

Tessa's tinkling laugh is infectious. "Good to know. No karaoke nights for you, then."

"Don't get me wrong, I love listening to music. I've even been known to dance—but people would pay me to stop singing if they heard me. You're lucky with our walls being so thin, I don't sing in the shower."

"I'll keep that in mind," Tessa muses as she takes another bite of her sandwich.

We finish our meal, making small talk and getting to know one another better. By the time we return to our four-plex, it feels as if no time has passed. However, my watch says differently. I'll barely be able to grab a quick shower and get to my first meeting on time. One thing is certain. I don't care how tired I am. I'm making an appearance to hear the live band tonight—especially if it means I have a chance to see Tessa again.

# Chapter 2
## Tessa

THIS MORNING WAS... interesting to say the least. Hannah and Pete waking me had nothing to do with it either. No—that'd be the way I can't stop thinking about Derek. There was just something about him that instantly put me at ease and had me opening up about things I hardly talk about.

Did Miss Mable put a truth serum in my latte? As I sipped, all I had to do was look at Derek and I found my life story pouring out. If it wasn't the latte, maybe it was the way his honey-colored eyes watched my every move, and I found myself needing to keep him talking. His voice alone did some-thing to my insides—and I swear—I've never seen such long lashes on a man. The way his eyes crinkled at the corners and his lips quirked, I just couldn't look away.

As soon as I step through the doors of my brewery, all thoughts of Derek disappear as my assistant manager approaches with wary eyes and pinched lips. That look alone tells me my day just took a turn for the worse.

*Fuck. What now?*

"Just so you know, everyone's all right," she blurts out. "But there was an incident."

Her only job is to be here when inventory arrives and to

make sure everything is ready when we open for the lunch rush at eleven. What could possibly go wrong?

As hard as it is not to probe her with questions, I wait for Kylie to explain.

"There was a new driver today making deliveries. Apparently, he didn't see our overhang and..." She pauses, and my gut clenches. Before I can say anything, she spews, "Well, I think we're gonna need a new gutter and some minor repairs to the building. I've already filed an incident report with the police, and I have all the information for their insurance company. You'll just have to reach out to get the ball rolling."

I have to see this for myself. Turning on a dime, I walk to the loading dock. With each step, I remind myself not to react —until it's warranted.

Nothing good will come of me freaking out.

Please let the dock still be functional and the expense be low.

Thankfully, Kylie knows me well enough to not say another word until I can determine my level of alarm. Pushing my way through the side door, I release the breath I didn't know I'd been holding, when I see for myself the damage isn't as bad as my wild imagination created. She's right, we'll definitely need a new gutter as it hangs haphazardly from the corner of the building. I'll have to get a few appraisals to determine the damage done to the building, but it should be easy to repair.

Realizing there's nothing I can do out here, I ask, "Do you mind calling Able Body Construction and ask Jimmy to see if they can get us a quote today for the damage? Or at least rehang the gutter so it doesn't cause more damage to the building?"

"Sure thing, Tessa. I would've called—but as no one was hurt, and I knew you'd be here within the hour. There was no need for you to rush over here."

"You did the right thing," I say on a sigh as I walk back inside. "Did Brayden say if our order of pears will be here in time to start that new batch next week?" I've got everything I need to make Pops's special brew, but Brayden's crops bring out the flavor the customers love. I'll wait for him rather than buy from anyone else. I only make this beer when pears are in season. It takes time and effort to get it just right, but it brings me back to my roots.

"Nope. Haven't heard from him. But I will reach out before I'm off shift." She pulls out her phone and makes what I assume is a note to remind herself.

This. Right here is why she's my assistant manager. I love that I can trust her to handle things when I'm gone. My first assistant manager called me for every little detail. Kylie may be two years younger than me, but she's got a strong work ethic and knows when I need to become involved. I'd trust her with my life. It's taken me nearly three years to find someone who loves this place as much as me and wants it to succeed. Without her, I wouldn't be living my lifelong dream. God knows, I'd need two of me to get everything done in a day to keep this place running. Trust me—at first, I tried—but burning the candle at both ends wasn't a feasible option long-term. I couldn't make the brew, open, and close the place seven days a week. Something had to give—and it came in the form of Kylie when I finally found her.

When the phone behind the bar rings, all thoughts of going home for a well-needed nap for the day disappear. My best daytime bartender can't get off the bathroom floor with the flu and sounds worse than death warmed over. He's not due for another hour, but I know without a doubt, I'll be right here into the night to keep things afloat as he was to pick up a double today to cover for another bartender on vacation through tomorrow.

So much for my meeting. I guess I'll have to call and reschedule.

Could this day get any worse?

LATER THAT EVENING, as I wait on a customer from behind the bar, the air shifts, and the hairs on the back of my neck tingle. Looking around to see what's the cause, I'm surprised when I lock eyes with Derek when he enters the crowded room. He's wearing an emerald button-down shirt, with the sleeves rolled to his corded forearms.

When did I start noticing arm porn from across the room?

"Miss?" the customer asks, clarifying if I've heard the order placed.

Fuck. I have no idea what this woman said.

"Uh. Sorry," I say as I mentally scold myself for being distracted.

"Can I get a vodka tonic and a pint of huckleberry wheat?"

Already starting to pour from the tap, I assure them, "No problem. Anything else?"

The tall man suddenly looks as if he's sucked on a lemon, rudely states, "No. Just these. I guess this is a serve yourself establishment." Implying his service hasn't been up to par.

Well, fuck you, too, buddy. We're slammed, and you had to wait your turn. Poor you. Anyone with a brain can see we have customers wall-to-wall in here and people sitting outside, too. Sure, we're down by two staff members, but what's left of us are doing the best we can. Of course, being the diplomatic business owner I am, I reply, "Here you go. Let me know if there's anything else you need."

He doesn't even thank me but grabs the drinks and makes his way to meet his party.

I don't give him a second glance as the next customer steps up and orders.

With the band about to start, everyone and their brother needs their drinks—now. Usually there's three of us behind the bar, but tonight, it's just me and Reagan, and I haven't had a second to breathe since the dinner rush came in earlier. Who am I kidding? I've been putting out fires all day since I walked in the door. The entire day's been a cluster fuck—not counting my breakfast with Derek—and I'm looking forward to a date with my pillow tonight.

After waiting on a few more customers, I notice Derek takes the only spot remaining at the bar. I hold up a finger to let him know I'll be with him momentarily, but he just waves me away, knowing I'm obviously busy. When the band starts their opening pitch, Derek swivels on his stool to listen.

"Hey, everyone. Thanks for being here tonight. I'm Shane, and this is Jared and John—and we're The Armorers." The room goes up in cheers, and I can't help but grin. Those boys deserve everything. Even if they did get their name from a freaking wrench set in the garage.

A few moments later, I hear my name being called out in thanks from the band. I quickly wave and get back to work. I love hot summer nights in Colorado. With the festival in town next week, everyone's either a tourist or the locals have come out of the woodwork to socialize. Either way, it's great for business, and I'm not complaining.

As the band plays their hearts out, the line at the bar dies down, so I make my way to Derek. "Hey, thanks for waiting. What can I get for you?"

"I'll try a pint of your Puckering Pear," he says with a smile that makes his dimple pop and my belly dip momentarily.

Ignoring my reaction, I nod. "Great choice. It's one of my personal favorites."

His smirk is almost sinful as he nods. "Glad it comes high on your approval list."

"It's a house specialty." Thanks to Gramps passing down his famous recipe.

"I'll take a B&B burger and fries while you're at it. Today's been crazy, and I haven't eaten dinner yet."

I can totally relate. "Sure. Just give me a minute to put your order in," I say as I input his order electronically to the kitchen. When that's done, I add, trying to make conversation, "Big day with meetings?"

On a long breath, he exhales, "Yeah. I revamped my entire

design and got three more ad campaigns ready to roll out this week. What about you? How has your day been?"

A complete and total shit show.

But he doesn't need to hear that. Instead, I simply shrug and admit, "I've been here since I left you."

He looks at his watch, and his eyes nearly bug out. "Do you always put in over twelve-hour days?"

"I do when people call in sick and someone's on vacation."

When his jaw remains dropped, I quickly add, "Those are the perks of owning the joint."

"I can admit, I'm the same way when a client needs something, especially since I'm now a one-man show. Please tell me you've at least eaten since this morning."

"I grabbed a sandwich before the dinner rush."

Before either of us can say anything, another customer approaches and places their order.

Derek chuckles sarcastically. "No rest for the wicked."

Ain't that the truth.

As I help my steady flow of staff and customers fill their drink orders, my eyes drift to Derek more than I'll ever admit. He's tapping a finger on the counter in beat with the rhythm with the band. He said he didn't sing... but I'm fairly certain he's a musician of some form. He's too in tune to the music not to be. Maybe he's a guitarist? Or drummer?

By the time I get around to checking on him again, his burger is long gone and pint empty. "Refill?" I ask, taking the glass from him.

"Sure. How long does the band usually play?"

"They're scheduled 'til eleven."

"I think you were right. You found a hidden gem with this group. I love their cover songs, but their original work blows me away."

Nodding in agreement, I smile at my inside joke with Nita. "Someday we'll be saying, I remember when I saw them play at that tiny bar in Bear Creek... look at them now."

"No kidding," Derek says as he looks back to the band. "Shane—their lead singer has an addictive sound."

"That's what I told Nita when I first heard them play. As much as I'll hate to see them go—I'm certain they won't be sticking around here for long."

Derek takes a swig of his drink then clears his throat. "Speaking of sticking around... I want to see more of the local sites. I'd love to book a fishing tour with a local and go white water rafting. Do you know which companies are best to go through?"

Before I can censor my thoughts, I practically shout, "Oh, hell no. Don't book a fishing tour. If you want to fish, I'll take you. As for rafting—check out Raven's Rapids. You'll get your most bang for your buck, and it'll be a blast. Tell them Tessa sent you, and you might even get a discount."

Derek's dark brow lifts as the edges of his mouth tip into a grin. "Good friend of yours?"

"Yeah. We went to school together. She's good people, and you gotta support the locals, ya know? Too many out-of-town rafting companies try to come in and pretend they're the experts. They usually crash and burn within a season or two. Raven's been on that river since she could walk. Her dad opened the company, and she's since taken over."

Derek pulls out his phone and types something into it, then stashes it away. "I've got it saved. I'll check them out tomorrow. But about that fishing..." he draws out as his eyes roam every inch of me. "Are you sure you have time?"

"I'm not sure about your schedule, but the fish bite early. My family has the best hole around, on our property. We do our best to keep it a secret, so don't be spreading rumors or anything. I'm off every Monday, so if you're interested, I'll meet you in the parking lot at five-fifteen a.m. It'll give us plenty of time to drive and set up."

Derek nods slowly. "That sounds perfect. Just tell me what I need to pick up in terms of gear, and we should be set."

"Did you bring a rod with you?"

Derek's cheeks darken, and his chagrin expression says he'll be buying whatever he needs. "Nope. I left that in Washington. But I can get whatever I need between now and then."

"No need. I've got everything at the house. Just bring yourself and whatever snacks you want. We'll stop for coffee on the way and..." I pause for effect. "If we're lucky, you'll be home by nine with a rainbow trout for dinner."

"You're that confident?"

"Do fish breathe underwater?" I spew from my lips before I can stop myself. I don't mean to be cocky, but I won't let him doubt me either.

He takes a long swig of beer, then on a long exhale, he nods. "Okay, then. I guess I'll be ready early Monday morning."

# Chapter 3
## Derek

"THE RIVER IS at the back of our property. The trees get thicker, and regular vehicles can't maneuver out there." With gear loaded in our arms, Tessa leads me to a side-by-side all-terrain vehicle meant for off-roading. She stashes our two cases with our rods, chest waders, and a backpack she claims to have all the gear we'll need, then points to where I can set the small backpack I brought with a few essentials for food.

The coffee we stopped for on the way out of town is kicking in, and I'm eager to see where this little adventure with Tessa takes me. She's sexy as fuck as she climbs in beside me as if she's driven this a million times and says with a devilish grin, "Buckle up, buttercup; it's gonna be a bumpy ride."

Buckling my five-point harness, I throw her sass right back at her, "So now you think I'm a buttercup... what did I do to you, to be called a toxic flower?"

Tessa's jaw drops, and she darts her eyes to mine incredulously. "What?"

"The buttercup plant contains a compound called protoanemonin. They're toxic to both humans and cows if eaten. Of course, they're harmless when dried out."

"Uh... okay, Mr. Encyclopedia. Good to know... I was just

trying to make you laugh…" Then mutters, "And obviously, it was an epic fail."

Oh, I laugh all right. My deep belly laugh fills the barn the ATV has been stored in. "You're adorable, Tessa, and I'm being an ass. Sorry. It's the response my sister gave me once when I used the same expression, and I've been dying to use it on someone else, to knock the wind out of their sails."

"I can honestly say, I've never heard that before. I guess you learn something every day. But fair warning. Two can play at that game." With that, she starts the ATV, puts it in gear, and we swiftly exit the barn. The ATV's lights are necessary, as the sun barely makes its presence known.

Chuckling, I mutter to myself, "I'll keep that in mind."

Tessa maneuvers the ATV like it's made for her. Her smile is infectious as she zips across the yard. At first, our path is smooth, but once we leave the maintained space, the terrain becomes rocky, and we bounce in our seats as she tries to take the smoothest path possible.

"Have you been fly-fishing before?" she asks as we hit a bump in the road, jerking us back in our seats.

"A few times. Though it's been years," I admit.

"Good, then we won't be starting from scratch. I'll show you what I know and set you up with all you'll need. With any luck, we'll have our limits in no time."

Ten minutes later, when we crest the top of the hill, I'm surprised to find the river off in the distance. Through the clearing in the Aspen trees, I barely make out the bluish bend, but it's there. Lined by rocks just beyond the trees. Now, the sun's fully up, making the water glisten. When Tessa brings the ATV to a stop in front of a big boulder, she turns to me with a triumphant grin. "Daylight's burning. Let's get moving, Derek."

Unbuckling her harness like a pro, she hops out of the ATV and reaches for a pair of waders. "Here, these should fit you. It's too damn cold to get wet. My dad wears a size thirteen, so I'm hoping your feet aren't bigger than his."

"Nope. We're good." My size elevens will fit with ease in those.

Instead of kicking off my shoes the way Tessa is, I find myself watching her. She's dressed in a pair of form-fitting jeans and an oversized hoodie. Her dark hair is windblown into a beautiful disarray. The sunlight magnifies the light sprinkling of freckles across the bridge of her nose, and her face is free of any makeup.

*Where else might she have freckles?*

Noticing my gaze trace over her body, she stops and raises her brow. "Something wrong?"

Shit. I'm totally busted.

Shaking off my thoughts of Tessa, I shrug. "Naw... I'm good."

Her blue eyes narrow on me as she scrutinizes my face. "You sure?"

Honesty pours from my lips. "In this light, your freckles show."

Brushing a finger over her nose, she briefly looks to her feet before locking her hypnotic gaze on mine. My pulse skips a beat as she sinks her teeth into her lower lip. Her expression is a cross between being coy and contemplating. "Yeah, they multiply like rabbits in the summer. I gave up long ago trying to cover them up."

Shocked she would ever feel the need, "Why?" bursts out. She's fucking gorgeous just the way she is. Why would she feel the need to cover her natural beauty?

"Teenagers suck," comes out as an exhausted sigh. "I hated being teased about them, but when I found a picture of my mom in high school and realize she could've passed as my twin, I stopped hiding who I was and wore them proudly. She was stunning in her photo, and I felt proud to be a part of her."

My chest tightens, remembering her loss. "No one should ever make you feel less—for any reason." I quickly learn Tessa's beautiful from the inside out, which only makes her more intriguing to me. Whoever says otherwise should have their head examined.

I'm caught off guard when her expression morphs from serious to a playful smirk. "Are you gonna keep staring, or are we fishing today?"

"Ah... you're a taskmaster. Got it." I smile coyly and shuck off one shoe. As I slip that leg into the waders and toe off my other shoe, I can't help but grin at Tessa. She pulls the straps over her shoulder and stuffs her oversized hoodie in at the waist. Then she fastens her inflatable life vest in place. She's completely outfitted in her insulated waders, yet in this moment, she couldn't be sexier. Her confidence is hot.

Before I can even get strapped into my waders, Tessa's already assembling a rod. Her teeth sink into her bottom lip as she starts at the tip of the rod and lines up the guide loops. Expertly, she starts it a quarter turn off, then twists the segments of the rod in place. She sure as fuck knows what she's doing because before I can even reach for the other case to get my rod, she sets hers against the ATV and reaches for it.

"Just because you're my official guide, doesn't mean you have to do all the work," I remind her. "I may be from Seattle, but I'm not a city slicker by any means. I can get my hands dirty and do the work right along with you."

"Be my guest." She shrugs what I think is an apology, but it's gone before I can process it further.

She hands me the tip of my rod, and I do my best to mimic her actions from only moments before, while she sets into stretching her line. I can't say I've ever been fishing with a woman outside my family—but if she's as efficient as she appears, we'll have our limits in no time.

With rods in hand, we walk to the riverbank. "From here until the bend is the best spot." She points to a spot about fifty yards away. "Unless you're really confident in your rolling cast, I'd recommend sticking to this side of the river, so you won't get your line stuck in the trees. You're welcome to cross, but this side is my preference. The water this time of year is only about hip deep on me, so you should be good either way."

"I'll stick to this side for now," I agree. I'm not ready to make a fool of myself unnecessarily. It's been a long minute since I've fly-fished. No need for any unnecessary malfunctions. Back home, I typically fish with a traditional rod, because the salmon and steelhead are stubborn buggers when they want to be, but when in Rome—as they say. Let's just hope I remember the tricks Pops taught me about rolling out my cast and getting into the perfect rhythm.

Thankfully, Tessa's not a mind reader, because all she does is nod. "Do you need any pointers? Or should I just step aside and let you do your thing?"

Not passing up the chance to watch Tessa, the words easily fall from my lips. "Why don't I watch you a few times, just to make sure I remember?"

After adjusting the bobber, the weights, and the imitation flies at the end of her line, Tessa steps to the edge of the water and faces upstream with one foot in front of the other. Then in a well-practiced move, she lets the slack into her line. Once she's certain she's got enough, she gracefully casts her line into the water and lets it flow downstream.

She rolls her line over the side and expertly casts it out. Instead of busying myself with my own line, I find myself watching her instead. In a rhythmic motion, her line flicks forward and back in line with the river. I swear not only is she sexy as fuck, but she's concentrating so hard, she's none the wiser of my staring.

Just as she casts it over her shoulder for the third time and lets it ride downstream a bit, her line snags in the water, and all the slack she had disappears in an instant. With grace and the patience of Job, she angles her rod and reels it in. Before I can even think to get off my ass and help, she's got her net out and has the beautiful rainbow trout unhooked from her line.

When her eyes meet mine, a wide grin spreads across her face. "It's gotta be at least ten pounds and will make a great supper."

"Are all the trout this big?" I ask in disbelief. The sucker has to be at least two feet long.

"They have to be a minimum of sixteen inches to keep, but this is one of the bigger ones we've pulled out of our property, that's for sure—and I'm not feeding you any BS either." After taking a few steps into the stream of water, she rinses off her hands and returns. "Okay, City Slicker, you ready to show me what you're made of?"

"I should've known I'd never live that comment down." I pretend to grumble as I walk away from where's she standing. Though the gleam in her eye has me not giving two fucks about the nickname. Tessa's a vixen and if she keeps looking at me like that, I might just have to kiss that smirk right off her face.

Not wanting to let my mind wander further about Tessa, I force myself to line up with the riverbank. Though I refuse to look, I can feel her stare as I let out some slack on my line. There's a crackle of energy that flows between us, I'm not quite sure how to describe, but I'm not entirely sure I want to let go of it either.

Slowly rolling back my line, I roll it forward in an attempt to emulate Tessa's actions while she saunters further up the bank. Trying my best to ignore her, I force my body and find the rhythm I need. Slowly, I cast forward and roll it back with ease, only to repeat the process at the end of my cast.

From the corner of my eye, I can't help but watch Tessa walk further up the bank and cast out again. I'm like a moth to a flame with that one. I've never been more thankful in this moment than to be standing behind her, so she doesn't catch me following her every move. Gingerly, she wades knee deep into the water as she finds her rhythm once again.

Over the trickling sounds of the riverbed, I hear Tessa yelp as she takes a step to steady herself, now thigh deep in the water. Her line is taut, and she steadily reels in another catch. Seriously, was her line even in the water a minute? She's either the luckiest person I've ever met, or she's a complete fish whisperer. Either way, I'm in fucking awe of how gracefully she lands another fish.

Abandoning my own line, I ask, "Need a hand?"

Tessa shakes her head as she grabs the net and scoops it up. "Thanks, but I've got it."

Once her fish is safely stowed with her other fish along the shoreline I call out, "Are you sure you're not using anything different on your line from what I've got set up?"

"Nope." She shrugs. "They're the same."

"Do you always land a fish in under a minute?"

Her eyes dance mischievously as she steps toward me, and my heart skips a beat.

"Aww... Derek, you're not jealous, are you?"

"In awe, more likely," I admit. "Are you sure you're not a fish whisperer or something?"

Tessa's head rocks back with laughter, and the beautiful sound carries louder than the water. "Hardly." She eventually guffaws. "It's not my fault you're not having any luck... though Gramps always said fishing is never about luck. It's pure talent and skill."

Feigning devastation, I place a hand over my chest as I cheekily ask, "Are you saying I have no skill?"

Reaching out to pat my cheek like she's consoling a small

child, she says, "We all have our talents, Derek. I'm sure you'll find yours."

That simple touch sends a jolt of electricity zinging through my body.

My dick jumps at the contact, and my gaze lands on her lips.

Lifting my hand to hold hers in place, I practically growl, "Oh, Tessa. I've got plenty of talents."

When her eyes pierce mine with a challenging stare, I could give two shits that I'm knee deep in a river with a rod in my hand. All it takes is her to apply the slightest bit of pressure against my cheek, pulling me toward her, and I step closer with ease, slanting my lips over hers.

When we're only a breath apart, Tessa raises an eyebrow and whispers, "You sure about that?"

My lips crash onto hers in an instant, and the electricity I felt from afar only intensifies.

She tastes of mint Chapstick and pure heaven. When she meets me with the perfect combination of push and pull as she opens her mouth to mine, my free hand reaches to the base of her neck to guide our kiss further. Her hand fists my Henley, pulling me closer. Words bubble from my lips without permission between kisses, "God... you feel... amazing."

Too involved in my kiss, I hardly notice the rod bob and pull away from me.

Tessa must though because she breaks our kiss and pants, "You've got a bite."

"What?" I ask, needing clarification. I may have let my teeth graze her lips, but I wouldn't say I'm biting her.

She points to my line in the water. "You've got a fish on."

"Fuck," I mutter. I didn't even notice.

Shaking my head, I clear my thoughts and reluctantly step away from her to reel in my catch. The fish gives its best fight as I angle my rod to get the most momentum in wrangling it in. Eventually, it's brought in. The entire time, I'm both elated and irritated. Of course, I didn't want to be skunked today, but if truth be told, I'd much rather spend the morning kissing Tessa than catching any number of fish.

Once I've got it in my net, I give Tessa a wide grin. "That's one way to get your luck to rub off on me."

Rolling her eyes as if that's the cheesiest line she's ever heard, she smirks. "Well... I have twenty bucks that says I'll limit out before you can even catch your next fish."

Rubbing my hand over my lips where they still taste of her, I quickly add, "You're certainly sure of yourself... I'll tell you what... You catch the next fish, and I'll clean the whole lot... but when I catch the next fish, you're gonna give me the chance to put my rod down and kiss you properly."

Reaching out, she grabs my shirt once again and pulls me close to her. Her eyes narrow on my lips and she lets her tongue dart out and slide along her bottom lip. Just when I think she's about to kiss me and give into the moment, she grins like the Cheshire cat and says, "If you're gonna make promises about your rod, you'd damn well better know how to use it."

With a wink, she bops me on the nose, turns on a dime, and saunters to the same spot she was before to cast out her line as if she didn't just rock my world mere seconds ago.

Staring at her like a fool, I can't help but wonder... What the fuck have I just gotten myself into?

# Chapter 4

## Tessa

DEREK LIVES up to his promise all right. When I snag my next fish before he can stop staring at me, his utter shock is priceless. With the taste of him on my lips, it takes every last ounce of control I have to walk away and cast out my line.

I've never had the luck I've displayed this morning. It's like I'm given a magical siren call to the fish, and they just can't stay away from my line. I have my limit in no time. Derek is a great sport, and our feisty banter continues until we return to our apartments. When he insists on frying my catch for dinner, I eagerly accept. After all—what's the point in cleaning a fish if you're not eating it?

Now, as I walk up the steps to meet him for dinner, my mind replays the moments leading up to our kiss this morning. Sure, I've always been a take what you want kind of girl, but with him losing our bet, I never got to experience what he considers a proper kiss, and I have to admit, I'm more than intrigued and a bit disappointed the situation never led itself for me to know firsthand if he could keep his promise.

My core clenches at the thought. Instinctually, my finger-tips brush over my once-swollen lips, remembering his taste. God, he felt amazing. I may have initiated our kiss, but he most certainly knew how to take control in a way that only turned me on further. I've seriously wanted to kick myself for not kissing him again before we parted ways earlier.

When I raise my hand to knock, the door swings open, taking me by surprise. "Oh, hey."

"Hey, yourself," he says on a lazy grin. I've never understood the phrase panty dropper more than I do in this moment. Who needs tequila to make your clothes come off, when Derek can melt my clothes away with a simple smile?

Fuck. Get it together, Tessa.

Yeah, he's sexually attractive.

Our chemistry is off the charts.

But I don't have time for relationships.

As I war with myself, he must say something I don't catch because he suddenly asks, "Tessa?" to get my attention.

Shit. What did he say?

"Everything okay?" he asks, his voice laced with concern.

"Yeah." I quickly dismiss my previous thoughts and focus on the delicious aroma wafting from his kitchen.

Beyond the obvious smell of fried fish, there's a sweet and savory scent I can't quite place, too. "Need any help with dinner?"

"I've just finished with the main course, and dessert will be finished any minute. I hope you don't mind I baked brownies, too. I've been craving them since I had one at a diner just outside of Salt Lake, so I thought I'd whip up some. Thank God this place came furnished, or I'd have been out of luck today. I didn't bring any pans."

He steps aside and gestures for me to enter his apartment. Knowing the layout is the same as mine, I find myself in the living room instantly. Though instead of a dining room table, there are only barstools at the bar bordering the kitchen where he gestures for me to take a seat while he finishes up.

"I picked up some Pinot Noir, would you like a glass?" he asks as he reaches for the bottle and holds up a glass.

"Sure, sounds great."

As soon as he hands me my glass, Derek plates the trout, alongside some asparagus and oven-baked red potatoes with herbs. I have no idea what I was expecting, but I'll admit, I'm impressed with the way he handles the kitchen with ease. I'm a functional cook at best. That's why I hired the best staff I can to run the kitchen at Bed Knobs & Brews. I may have the ideas —like offering organic choices on the menu—but my specialty is the brew itself.

His leg brushes against mine as he sits beside me, causing tingles to rush up my spine. Ignoring my body's reaction to him, I take a sip of wine and focus my attention on the plate of food in front of me. "Do you cook often?"

Derek lets out a heavy breath and admits, "Well, I'd rather not live on takeout, so I cook out of necessity. I've long outgrown the ramen and prepackaged meals phase of my life."

Something about the way he says it has me fighting to hold back a smile. "I get it."

"Mom always made sure we could fend for ourselves. She had heard about her friends' kids going off to college, not even knowing how to boil water to make the ramen. So, from a young age, we were asked to help in the kitchen."

"Being from Seattle, do you eat fish a lot?"

Shaking his head, he chortles. "No. Contrary to popular

belief, people in Seattle eat a variety of foods that don't involve seafood. When we're at my grandparents', yes. It was a tradition in our family. But I actually grew up outside of Leavenworth. There were lakes and rivers around, but we were in the mountains, not close to the ocean."

"Oh, I've heard of that place. It's the one that looks like a small German Village, right?" I remember watching a show about it on some travel channel growing up with my grandmother.

"Yep. That's the one. My parents own and run a store in Cashmere, a town close by. But that's essentially where I grew up."

"Did you work at the store growing up?"

"Yep, every summer until I started doing internships for college. My parents have four kids, and all of us have taken different paths that led us out of town as we grew up."

I've lived here my entire life. I can't imagine living away from my family. "Do you see your family often?"

"Yeah, it's only a couple of hours' drive from where I live. It would be a drop in the hat for you, since all the major cities around here are so spread apart," he teases as he forks a piece of asparagus.

"True." He's not lying. If you want to go to any major shopping center, you have to travel almost forty-five minutes. But you get used to it, or you shop local. "Where do your siblings live now?"

"Dani and Luke live between his loft in Tacoma and his home on Anderson Island. It depends on his work schedule. But since she's an author, she can write from anywhere. Davis is in med school at OHSU in Portland, and oddly enough, my brother Damien just moved closer to him and is working on Columbia River University's campus at the moment."

"Is he a professor?"

"Oh, God, no. He's a civil engineer and is in charge of a big housing project."

"Wow, you certainly have spread out then. I can't imagine living far away from my dad, since he's the only family I have left... though with him on the road, I guess he does more than enough traveling between the two of us."

"True. But like you, traveling doesn't bother my family. In fact, my brothers and Dani will be coming here in a few weeks so we can watch the season opener between Denver and the Rainier Renegades."

"I knew you were too good to be true." I pretend to pout.

"Why is that?" he asks as his brows shoot to his hairline.

"You're a Rainier Renegade fan... I'm Denver all the way."

Derek's deep laugh fills the room. "I'm sure you'll survive. Though I'd be tossed out of the family if I ever converted."

"Die-hard sports fans?"

A deep rumble of laughter fills the room. "Yeah... and the fact that my sister just married Luke Leighton. With him being the head coach of the Renegades, it'd be a little hard to show up at family functions."

"Wait. Your sister is Charlotte Ann? I thought you said her name was Dani?"

Derek cringes and completely ignores my question. "You've read her books?"

Why is he cringing? "Yeah?" Comes out as a question

because she's a fucking amazing author. Why wouldn't I read her books? "Haven't you?"

When Derek's cheeks darken, I'm surprised when he whispers, "No."

"Why not?" I ask incredulously.

"For starters, she asked us not to."

"What?" comes out before I can think of a reason for myself. That's strange. Wouldn't she want them to support her?

"Since we're her brothers, and she writes romance, she made a rule when Davis and Damien were still in high school that we couldn't read her books. She didn't want to corrupt their young minds, her words—not mine. She didn't want them learning about sex from her stories. We've all purchased the books, but to my knowledge, we haven't read them."

"Thinking about some of the sexier scenes in a few of her stories, I guess I can see why. Definitely not something I'd want my little brothers reading—however, my roommate in college introduced those books to me, and we totally loved them."

"Seriously? Are they that sexy? I just thought she was giving them a hard time."

"There's sex in them—and don't get me wrong—it's hot. But your sister is extremely talented and tells a wonderful story, too."

"I'm sure she is, and I'll take your word on that. But I made a promise to her when she made the littles promise... and I'm not going back on my word."

"The Littles?" What the hell is he talking about?

Rolling his eyes, he grins. "It's what Mom used to call my two younger brothers. Dani and I were the bigs, while Dame and Davey were the littles. It started out when they were too young to do anything, and it just kind of stuck. Yeah, they're practically full-grown men now, but they're still the littles in our family. Sorry—force of habit."

"Being an only child, I'm always fascinated by the dynamics of large families."

Not wanting my food to get cold, I take a bite of his seasoned potatoes, and an uncontrollable moan escapes. "This is delicious, Derek. I could eat the entire pan of these."

"Thanks, there's more here when you're ready." He takes a bite from his own plate and nods in agreement. "This does taste good."

After each of us take a few more bites of this mouthwatering food, Derek breaks the silence. "So, tell me more about this USA Music Festival this weekend. I've seen signs everywhere, and you mentioned it's a pretty big thing."

"It's the biggest event this town will see all year. It's a lot like other major music festivals. I guess you could compare it to Bonnaroo or Lollapalooza. Music starts Friday around noon and plays through Sunday. There's an amphitheater for the big headliners and about eight other stages in grassy areas where over one hundred bands will play throughout the weekend."

"I... uh.. didn't expect it to be that big. I'm sure I've missed any chance of scoring tickets this late. Some of the names mentioned are big."

"Yeah, it's been sold out for some time... but if you play your cards right, I might have an extra ticket you can score."

*Score? Did I just say that?*

"Oh, really?" His tone is playful, and his eyes darken. When he leans closer to me, capturing my undivided attention, the scent of his cologne captures my senses. All I can think about is what his lips felt like on mine. "Just what would I have to do to earn said tickets?"

*Kiss the ever-loving fuck out of me like you did this morning?*

"Uh…" My words get trapped in my head as I stare at his perfect lips. His five o'clock shadow has made an appearance, and it takes everything in me not to reach out and run my fingertips along his stubble.

"I can see your mind spinning. What's going on in there?"

*Oh, Derek. You have no idea.*

"As one of the local sponsors, I have a booth set up to push my latest and most popular microbrews. But I have two all-access tickets to the entire event. Originally, I'd planned to take Nita, my best friend. Last month, her grandma surprised her with a trip to Venice for her birthday. There's no way she'd ever turn down a trip like that—and more importantly, time with her grandma. Besides, we go to the festival every year."

"Are you working the event?" Derek asks with interest.

"I'll have to check in with my employees, but between the Bed Knobs and the festival, I've got plenty of staff hired and trained for this weekend. In fact, I have a crew that only does local festivals on a temporary basis. They like the steady jobs in the summer, and the flexibility to only work weekends. It's a win-win for us all."

"Wow. I hadn't realized you'd expanded your business

beyond the storefront. That's amazing. If you don't mind me asking, what made you choose microbrewing?"

I smile proudly at the memory. "My grandfather."

"How so?" Derek asks as he turns his body closer to me.

"Well, Gramps was actually part of the Bear Creek Runners back in the days of prohibition."

"Seriously?"

"Yeah, Colorado was dry from 1916 to 1933. Gramps was born in 1917. When he was thirteen, he started running moonshine and specialty brews. His dad had been doing it and figured no one would give any thought to a teenager being a runner. That's actually how we ended up with our property. My great-grandfather had come to Bear Creek as a miner back in 1910, but when alcohol was banned, he saw a way to profit from it. He passed it down to Gramps, who passed it to my dad. Eventually, I guess it will be mine. Some of the outbuildings are where I started making brew and still do to this day—in a larger capacity. I learned everything I know, thanks to Gramps."

"You said he was born in 1917? How old was he when he passed?"

It takes me a minute to do the math. "He died in 2010. He'd just turned ninety-three."

Derek's brows shoot to his hairline. "You're what? Twenty-six? Were you making brew before you could walk?"

"No, but close. Gramps never stopped making it. I guess I was ten when I took a real interest. Living with him, it was just something we did to pass the time when I wasn't in school for the summer."

"You were drinking at ten?"

"Hell, no. Sure, I tasted it from time to time—to make sure it was up to par. But they made me wait until I was twenty-one before I actually had a full glass of my own—that was Grandma's demand."

"Okay, that makes sense. But how did you go from making beer with your grandpa, to owning an entire brewery?"

Fair question. "When it was just Gramps and me, he used to tell me all sorts of stories and predicaments he got himself into as a kid. Grandma would have a fit when she found out—she didn't want him being a bad influence on me... so we kept it between the two of us."

When I see Derek's expression change, I blurt out, "Don't get me wrong, she loved Gramps and was proud of his past; she just wanted to make sure I went to college first to pursue other options. I wanted to keep our family recipes alive. I also wanted to create some of my own because I always loved experimenting."

"That's incredible," Derek says as he places a hand on my knee.

"Part of the stipulation in my inheritance when Gramps passed, was that I had to graduate from college before I could use the money he'd put aside to open a microbrewery. They wanted to make sure I was following my dreams—not theirs."

"They would be so proud of what you've accomplished."

"Yeah," I say with a sigh, thinking of Gramps' infectious smile. "That Puckering Pear you drank the other night was one of his favorites right before he passed. He worked for ages to perfect the recipe. It always makes me smile when we finish another batch."

"I'm sure it does. I loved it. In fact, I was wishing I'd bought a growler to have some the other night when I wanted a beer to relax after a taxing day with clients. Next time I won't make that mistake."

Reaching for his hand, I give it a squeeze. "Well... I have an in with the owner. I'm sure we can make that happen soon for you."

"I think knowing the owner has a lot of perks." He smirks, causing my libido to rev like I've just stepped on the accelerator to a muscle car. My core clenches, and I have to press my thighs together to gain some relief, but it's pointless.

"Is that so..." I say, playing his game.

Derek's free hand brushes the hair from my face and he traces his palm against my cheek. "Well..." he draws out as his hand shifts to the base of my neck. "For starters, if I didn't know her, I wouldn't be able to smell your delicious scent..."

Leaning in, he pauses right before our lips meet. On instinct, my lips part in anticipation.

His voice is deeper and the sexiest I've ever heard when he whispers, "I also wouldn't be able to do this..."

When his lips press onto mine, every nerve in my body responds. He may have started the kiss as sweet and sensual, but when I return it, I take it to an entirely new level. My hands reach for his face where I finally give into my temptation and trace along his jawline and into his silky dark hair.

He feels fucking incredible. His cologne has been toying with my senses since I arrived and now that I'm able to get up close and personal with him, I only want him more. When my fingers graze along the back of his neck, he turns my stool so my entire body faces his.

When his legs entangle with mine, the warmth from his body only fuels my need from him. When his hand roams down my back, pressing me closer to him, I almost fall off my stool.

Breaking our kiss, he stammers, "Shit. Are you okay?"

*I'm more than okay. I need to kiss you some more.*

But instead, I say, "I'm good."

Glancing at our almost empty plates, he asks, "Are you still hungry?"

For you? Yes. "For food?"

A loud chortle fills the room. "Yes."

"Um..." Glancing at my half-eaten plate, I feel a bit guilty for having no interest all of a sudden. "Not really."

Just then, the buzzer for the brownies goes off, and we both jump in surprise.

Quickly pressing his lips to mine, he whispers, "Hold that thought. I'll be right back."

All I can do is stare at his sexy ass as he bends to remove the brownies from the oven. He's wearing a pair of well-worn jeans that fit his muscular body perfectly. Between that and the fitted black tee stretching across his back, my mouth goes dry.

After turning off the oven, he turns and catches me staring.

The fire in his eyes tells me he's no longer hungry for food.

No—as he strides purposely around the counter, keeping eye contact, he has only one thing on his mind—me.

When he stops in front of me, he reaches for my hand, and I stand.

"I believe we were interrupted," he says as he guides my face to his.

"I wasn't quite done with you yet," I admit.

"Well, we wouldn't want that," he says as he licks his lower lip right before pressing a searing kiss onto mine. Fuck. He feels amazing. But he pulls back all too soon.

Tilting his head to the living room, he asks, "What do you say we continue this on the couch?"

I'm all for not falling off the stool and making a fool of myself. But instead of responding, I simply take his hand and walk in that direction.

I don't even make it to the couch before his arms snake around my waist from behind, and he kisses the back of my neck. When he reaches that spot just behind my ear that drives me wild, I moan.

"I love learning your body," he whispers between kisses as his teeth graze my outer lobe, making my panties melt and my core clench in anticipation. Fuck, if he has me reacting like this in just a few simple moves, I'm in it for when he actually touches me where it counts.

Slowly, he spins me so that I'm facing him, and our lips meet once again. As if they have a mind of their own, my hands skirt under the hem of his shirt, and I finally get to see for myself what his skin feels like. They trace up his spine and when I realize there isn't much give in the material, I reluctantly break our kiss, panting. "Take this off."

Derek's grin is devilish as he practically growls, dragging

his shirt over his head. "Okay, then. But two can play this game."

His hands reach for my waist, but he doesn't even have to ask. I reach for the hem of my tank and rip it over my head. "That better?" I raise a brow in challenge.

Running a hand down his face, he murmurs, "Fuck... You're beautiful."

"Right back at ya..." I smirk. As his eyes roam over my body, they land on my chest. Is it possible for one look alone to make them feel heavier as he takes them in? Thank God, I'd gone for a black demi-cup bra that accentuates my breasts perfectly.

Pulling me so we're suddenly chest-to-chest, his body feels incredible. The pressure against my breasts sends an ache to my core. When he bends to kiss along my collarbone, my clit strums to the beat of my increasing heart rate. He's barely begun to touch me, and I'm already gearing up to shoot off like the Fourth of July. What the actual fuck? How does he do this to me?

Needing to regain control, I rake my short nails along his back and murmur, "Lie down."

# Chapter 5
## Derek

"LIE DOWN," Tessa says as she scrapes her nails along my back.

The heat in her eyes and the tone of her voice has my dick straining against my jeans. The searing look she gives me as she pushes against my chest has me willing to let her take the lead—for now.

When the back of my calves hit the couch, I twist so I can do as she asks.

To my extreme pleasure, she straddles my jean-clad legs and runs her soft hands along my chest. She's sitting just below my raging dick, but if she were to lie on top of me, she would know in an instant just what she does to me.

At first, I try to keep my hands clenched at my sides, but when she bends forward and kisses a trail from my abs to my collarbone, all bets are off. My hands slip to the side of her waist and trail back and forth as she takes exactly what she wants from me.

When her lips finally make it to my mouth, I devour her. My hands roam over her body. I can't get enough of her. When her teeth scrape against my lower lip, my hands cup her ass and pull her closer. Through our clothes, her hips gyrate as if she's slowly dry humping me and fuck, it feels amazing.

Needing to give her more, I cup her breast and squeeze, causing the most exquisite moan to fall from her lips. When she traces kisses to my ear, I unhook her bra, letting her perfectly round breasts fall free to my face. Needing to taste them, I kiss my way down her neck and take one plump nipple into my mouth, while applying pressure to the other.

I can tell she likes it because she squirms against my cock and moans. I take that as a cue to double down on my efforts. Sucking on her nipple, I take more into my mouth and play my tongue along the tip. Fuck, she likes this. Her hips grind into mine through our clothes, and I need to move her off my dick, or I'm going to do something I haven't done since I was a teen.

Slipping my hand away from her breast, I trail my fingers along her body, until I find the hem of her shorts. Instinctually, she rises on her knees, allowing room for my fingers to slip up the leg of her shorts and trace along the edge of her panties.

Fuck, she's soaked.

Which only turns me on further.

Sliding my fingers under the edge of her panties, I lazily trace my fingers along the line from her slit. I'm rewarded with the most magnificent sound. It's a cross between a moan and a growl.

"Harder..."

Not sure what she means, I suck harder, pinch, and quicken my pace at her core. When her hips buck against my hand, I find her center with my middle finger and slip it inside.

"Yes... like that..." She's barely audible, but I get the point.

Giving a come-hither motion with my finger, my thumb finds her clit and circles it. Instantly, she rides my hand harder.

When I press against her upper wall that's just above her pelvic bone, she may as well speak in tongues. I flick her clit, once, twice... and her body clenches like a vise grip on my finger.

"So close..."

"Come for me, Tessa," I growl as I pull her nipple further into my mouth, flicking it with my tongue in the same motion as I strum her clit. Mere seconds later, I'm rewarded when her body stiffens. When a scream forms in her throat, she stifles it by biting my shoulder.

I gasp at the unexpected pain, but the way she's milking my hand, I could care less. Tessa is so beautiful in this moment. Letting her ride my hand until she's turned into a puddle on top of me.

Her head falls onto my chest as she pants heavily.

Slipping my fingers from her core, I trace my fingers along her spine as her breathing returns to normal.

Eventually, she lifts her head and peers at me with her electric-blue eyes.

"You okay?" I ask, making sure I didn't take things too far.

"More than okay," she says with a lazy grin.

"You're so fucking beautiful," I whisper. "Though next time you come, I want it on my tongue."

"Oh, I think I can handle that," she challenges. "But, first, I have something else in mind."

She presses up, and my body instantly misses her touch.

Without a word, she closes the distance between us and kisses me. When her tongue sweeps over mine, my dick jumps to full attention against the leg she's resting between my thighs.

Suddenly, she breaks our kiss and talks directly to my cock as she squeezes it through my jeans. "Oh, don't worry, I haven't forgotten about you."

Not wanting her to feel obligated, I roll my eyes. "You can just ignore him. He's an attention whore and will settle down if you leave him be."

Raising a brow, Tessa challenges, "What if I don't want to ignore him?"

Reaching down, she cups my balls through my jeans and squeezes lightly.

Well, fuck.

It's not what I had planned for tonight... but who am I to complain.

"Tessa, you don't have to..." I start, but she places a finger against my lips.

"Shh... I don't *have* to do anything. But this is something I've been dying to do, so let me."

Her eyes never leave mine as she challenges me to stop her from popping the fly of my jeans and slowly lowering my zipper. Damn. Her determination is hot as hell. If she keeps this up, she won't even have to touch me, and I'll be disgracing myself in an instant.

As soon as the fly is down, she tugs on my jeans, and my cock springs to attention, jumping to meet her eagerly. With a grin, she slowly traces me from root to tip. Fuck, her soft finger feels out of this fucking world. I want nothing more than to be inside that tight pussy, but by the look Tessa has on her face, it's clear she has other plans when she darts her tongue out to moisten her lips.

She's like a wet dream that's come to life.

She slides down my body and settles between my legs. To give her more room, I sit up and let one leg rest on the floor. For a long moment, she simply stares into my eyes as she strokes me, making me grow harder with each pump. Then she kisses down my abdomen as she cups my balls, giving them a gentle squeeze.

The moment her lips touch the head of my cock, I take in a sharp breath involuntarily as electricity zips up my spine unexpectedly. Her tongue circles the tip as her palm finds my shaft, making me groan in pleasure. "God, you feel amazing."

With a wicked smile, she licks me from root to tip, and my hips buck under her, causing her to laugh in appreciation. "Oh, I'm just getting started, Derek."

"If this is just getting started, I'm gonna be dead before this is done."

*Fuck. What the hell is she doing to me?*

The next time she circles my tip with her tongue, she takes me into her mouth, and my cock presses against the back of her throat. "Hmmm.... So good..." I moan as my eyes roll to the back of my head in pleasure.

She fists the base of my shaft and finds the perfect rhythm of push and pull that has me on the edge of no return much sooner than I'd ever expect. Each time she gets to my tip, her tongue circles the head before she uses the perfect amount of suction to get her lips to meet her fist along my shaft.

Sparks fly up and down my spine and before I know it, they invade my vision. Stroke for stroke, she applies the perfect amount of suction and pressure, and I fucking see stars.

Tapping her shoulder to give her a warning, I pant out, "I'm so close, Tessa."

She sucks harder and presses that spot right behind my balls.

The next thing I know, I empty myself into her. "Oh... fuck me... I'm coming..."

My eyes roll into the back of my head as she sucks down every last drop.

Pulling her on top of me, she laughs as she says, "Okay, then."

Not quite processing her words, my eyes pop open to make sure we're okay.

"What did you say?" I ask for clarification.

"You said to fuck you. Next time you come, that's how it's happening."

I seriously must be drunk on an orgasmic high. She didn't just say that. Did she?

"Wha...?" I start, but she cuts me off.

"I said..." She pauses to get my full attention. "I said, the next time you come, I'll be fucking you."

What do I even say to that?

I swear, this woman is fucking made for me.

Pulling her closer to my mouth, I crash my mouth onto hers. She tastes of Tessa and me, and I can't get enough.

"Be careful what you wish for, Tessa," I tease when we finally break to catch our breaths. "You may get more than you bargained for."

As challenging as ever, she simply smiles deviously. "Promises... promises..."

# Chapter 6
## Tessa

AS I GET ready for the music festival, I'm still thinking about my time with Derek this week. We still technically haven't had sex, but I can't tell you the number of times we've made each other come in the hottest makeout sessions imaginable. Don't get me wrong, I've had sex-only relationships—but with Derek, there seems to be more—and I'm not sure what to make of it. We've seen each other almost every day, either for coffee in the morning before his meetings, for dinner at Bed Knobs when I'm working, or when I get off work late in the evenings.

Being with him, I find myself more adventurous than ever. With a simple touch, he lights me up from the inside out. But there's more to him than that. He wants to spend just as much time with me outside the bedroom, getting to know each other —hence the reason we haven't actually had sex yet.

Knowing we'll be at the festival all day, I apply sunscreen and SPF Chapstick as well as throw a hoodie into the bag I've packed with a blanket to sit on.

Normally, I don't give much thought to my outfit, but I'll be spending the day with Derek, and I've taken some extra efforts. I'm wearing my favorite pair of dark-green shorts and my black top with the peek-a-boo sleeves to show off my half-sleeve tattoo. It fits me perfectly, accentuating my boobs in a way that's flattering but not too revealing. Glancing in the mirror one last time, I tease my hair to keep it out of my face. It's the perfect combination of sexy and sass.

When Derek knocks on my door, he instinctively gives me a once-over, letting me know I've made the right choice. His lips pull into a grin when he leans in to give me a quick kiss. "You look amazing, Tessa."

I take a moment to appreciate him as well. He's wearing a pair of black cargo shorts and a Rainier Renegades tee. "You do realize we're in Colorado, right?" I tease.

"Yep, but no matter what you do, you'll never convert me into a fan of Denver. You may as well give up now." He kisses me once more. "You ready?"

"Yeah, let me get my bag."

When I return, he reaches for my hand as if he's done it a million times and takes me to his Range Rover. I shouldn't let him get the wrong impression—I don't do long-term, serious relationships. I don't have time to put the effort into them, but I'm not done with Derek yet. There're still so many things we haven't tried, and I'm not even close to having my fill of him. He's so easy to be around. He makes me laugh, is challenging, and does spectacular things to my body I didn't even know were possible. Besides, he's new in town and doesn't know anyone, and we're just hanging out.

I'll admit it feels weird not working on one of my busiest days of the year, but Kylie assured me it isn't necessary. She has things handled at Bed Knobs and Marek, my special event manager, has things handled for the festival. It took a while not to micromanage everything—as this was my baby, but I'm finally able to just check in and walk away, from time to time.

When Derek pulls into the festival, I hand him my special vendor's parking pass. The festival itself opened a few hours ago, so the place is packed. We hear music in the distance and feel excitement in the air. I love all types of music and from what Derek has said, he does, too—so today should be fun.

The plan is to check in with Marek first and make sure he doesn't need anything before roaming the rest of the festival. The only thing on my agenda today is to get decent seats for one of my favorite bands performing tonight. There's no way I'm missing them.

My dad is a die-hard country fan. When we discovered The Whiskey Barrels—an alternative country band, we finally found something we could blast and enjoy when I rode along with him on some of his long-haul trips. Usually I only went once each summer, as I didn't enjoy being stuck in his rig for days on end. But Dad always made sure we stopped some-where new and exciting, so it was worth my torture.

Once we're inside the festival, I hear a deep voice call my name. "Tessa? Is that you?"

I'd recognize the voice anywhere, and my heart races as I turn in excitement.

"Jace? Is that really you?" Rushing toward him, I throw my arms around his neck and hug the hell out of him. "Where the hell have you been? I haven't seen you in years."

Chuckling, he releases me. "The Navy keeps me on their schedule. When my parents moved to Glenwood Springs, I spend my limited time there—not in Bear Creek."

"Wait... Navy? I thought you were at Princeton." But now that I look at him, he's completely changed. He's gained about thirty pounds of pure muscle and is definitely all man. A lot has changed in eight years, that's for sure.

Grinning wide, he says, "Let's just say, they made me an offer I couldn't refuse."

Offer he can't refuse? What the hell does that mean? "Did you even graduate?"

He was the first in his family to go to college, so I know how important it was for him to go to school.

"Yes—Bossy pants. I did." He smirks. "At the top of my class even. As a freshman, I joined ROTC, then joined the Navy and became a SEAL."

"What the hell? Why don't I know any of this?" I'm obviously a shit friend.

"I don't have social media—and last I heard, you've been busy setting up Bed Knobs & Brews."

"How the hell do you know that? We haven't spoken in years?" I ask in disbelief.

On a sly grin, he says, "Oh, I have my ways."

Just then, Derek clears his throat, drawing our attention. "Oh, shit. Sorry. Jason, this is Derek. Derek, this is Jason." Turning to Derek, I ask, "Do you remember me telling you about that boy I punched in first grade? Well, this is him. Besides Nita, this knucklehead was my best friend growing up. But when he went off to college, I thought he forgot all about us. We were like the Three Musketeers growing up."

"I'd never forget about you, T. But I've..." He trails off. He looks to Derek then back to me. "Been busy."

"Well, I'm so glad to be blessed with your presence..." I pretend to snark.

The shithead ignores me and focuses his attention on Derek. "Derek, I don't believe we've met. Are you new in town?"

"Uh, I just introduced you," I remind him and hope he doesn't get into his protective ways and be a dick to Derek. I'm twenty-six, not sixteen. He's like the older brother I never wanted when it comes to me dating. "But for your information, *Jace*," I say his name in warning. "He's just moved to town and happens to be my upstairs neighbor." God, why do I feel like I'm back in high school again?

Jace reaches out his hand to shake Derek's.

"Nice to meet you," Derek says.

"You, too," Jace says. "You're a Rainier Renegades fan. I take it you're from Washington?"

"Seattle." Derek nods.

Out of nowhere, Jason's little sister appears. Gosh, she must be nearly eighteen by now. She's grown so much since I last saw her. "Jace, are you ready yet? You promised me we'd be on time to see The Flower Petals. You know they're my favorite band. I can't miss it. I'm supposed to meet Brennan. Let's go."

Jace sighs heavily, and his disdain for Brennan is evident. God, I know that look so well. He pulled it on me and every single guy I dated in high school. I almost feel sorry for his sister.

"Hey, Tessa. How are you?" Melanie says when she recognizes me and reaches out for a hug. I used to babysit her all the time when Jace was busy. Hell, my dad even had me stay with them a few times after my grandparents passed. But when they moved away after graduation, we lost touch.

"God, you look amazing, Mel. Are you a senior next year?"

Proudly, she grins. "Yep. I've already been accepted to the University of Colorado, but I'm waiting to hear from a few others before I commit."

"I'm so happy for you, Mel."

Apologetically, she shrugs. "We do need to go, Jace. The concert starts in fifteen minutes. Give me your number, Tessa, and we'll have to catch up." She pulls out her phone and opens the screen for me to input my number.

Giving them each one last hug, I warn, "Don't be strangers. I expect to hear from the both of you—soon." They both agree, and Mel tugs Jace away as quickly as he had arrived. They disappear into the crowd.

When I turn back to Derek, I can't read his expression. Instead of reaching for my hand the way he easily had before, I find his hands stuffed in his pockets. But he manages to find a smile and asks, "Ready to check on your booth?"

Maybe I'm reading this wrong.

"Sure," I say, shrugging off my moment of unease.

It doesn't take long before we're at Bed Knob's booth. It's early, but customers are steady. When Marek spots me, he says, "Hey, Tessa. How's it going?"

"Good. Just checking in. Do you all need anything before I head off to a concert?"

Marek's in his late twenties and is a middle school teacher here in town. He and his new wife are just starting out and being my events manager was a perfect fit for him. Most of the jobs are for the weekends or during the summer. He used to be a bartender in college and knows his way around a microbrew like a pro. We've established that he hires his own seasonal crew and manages the staff for these events. Of course, I have final say in everything and pitch in when needed, but Marek keeps me from stretching myself too thin. By having Marek and his event team, it also brings more business to Bed Knobs & Brews throughout the year. Once they taste my specialty drinks, they always come back.

NOT WANTING to make the same mistake twice, I quickly introduce Marek to Derek. Marek has never met a stranger and easily makes small talk with Derek. Derek's shirt makes him a dead giveaway that he isn't a local, so Marek quickly finds out what brings Derek to town. While they talk, I quickly stash my bag under the counter and do a quick inventory to see if there's anything missing. Of course, there isn't. But old habits die hard.

When I'm back, Marek raises a brow. "Everything up to your standards?"

Rolling my eyes, I grin. "Of course. Everything's better than expected. You're doing a fantastic job, Marek, and I'd be lost without you. You tell that wife of yours I'd better see her soon."

"Raya's working on getting her master's degree this summer. But I'll be sure to bring her by when I know you're working for dinner."

"Sounds good." I look around and realize I'm truly not needed. "Well, if you need anything, you know where to find me. Derek and I are catching a few concerts this afternoon while we wait for Whiskey Barrels to perform. I left my bag here, so I don't have to tote it all afternoon. But I'll try to keep out of your hair."

"Sounds like a plan." Then he turns to Derek. "It was great meeting you, man. Enjoy the festival."

Derek and I spend the day enjoying the bands. We've listened to everything from metal to country. So that we don't miss The Whiskey Barrels, Derek and I make sure we show up for the opening act, Riser. I've seen them play before, and they're pretty good. The lead singer, Nick Conners, looks a bit like Sam Hunt, but his voice is all his own. I love the energy and the vibe Joel, their lead guitarist, and Nick have when they get in the groove.

When Riser's set is over, I'm buzzing with energy. I can't wait for Hardy West, the lead singer of The Whiskey Barrels, to make an appearance. I hope I can get a good enough picture to send to my dad, who's traveling to Salt Lake today. After listening to an assortment of music all day, I'm eager to hear their familiar songs.

Derek and I manage to score a spot near the right side of the stage for general admission. It'll be standing room only during the performance, I'm sure. But that's a risk I'm willing to take. I can't watch them perform and not be as close as possible.

Knowing there's still time before The Whiskey Barrels perform, I excuse myself to use the restroom. Derek offers to wait outside for me, but I assure him I'll be fine. Besides, I don't want to lose our seats.

As I stand in line waiting to use the restroom, I glance at the men's room. Of course, there's never a line there. When I've been standing for about ten minutes, I feel my phone vibrate, notifying me of a text.

**Derek: Okay—Total truth—I've written and erased this message at least five times, and there's no way for this to not sound weird—but are you okay? You've been gone awhile, and I feel weird for checking on you—but would hate myself if I didn't check in—and something was wrong.**

My chest tightens at his thoughtfulness, and I giggle at his rambling. It means a lot that he'd want to check on me—but that had to be awkward as fuck to write when you know your date is in the bathroom. To put him out of his misery, I quickly tap out a message.

**Me: I haven't fallen in—or been abducted. One of the perks of being a girl is long-ass lines for the bathroom. I'm still waiting in line.**

**Derek: I heard that is a hazard in public places. Glad you haven't fallen in. I will let you pee in peace. (And now I feel like a preteen talking about toilets. Great... I'm making a stellar impression— I'm sure)**

**Me: (smiley face emoji) We're good. There's at least five more people ahead of me. So, it may be awhile longer. If I'm ever in charge of the world, there will be three times more women's toilets in each venue than what is currently in place.**

**Derek: Good to know.**

By the time I can return to Derek, I'm surprised to see him talking with a woman.

She's talking animatedly with her hands, while Derek listens attentively.

A genuine smile plays at his lips as he runs a hand through his hair.

She hands him something, and he slips it into his wallet.

My stomach dips as I watch her throw her arms around Derek. She hugs him tightly—which he clearly reciprocates.

I've been on the receiving end of those hugs. She smiles as she steps away. Derek always leaves me smiling, too. The way his scent lingers, and my insides feel gooey. With just one look, he has me turned on in a nanosecond.

Seriously? Have I entered an alternate universe?

I'm fantasizing about Derek while he's looking at another woman?

Maybe I'm reading this wrong.

But when I get within hearing distance, the woman clearly says, "Now that you have my number, you'd better get in touch with me when you get back to Seattle."

What the fuck? Did I really just hear that right? He's on a date with me and asking someone else out?

The better question is why do I care?

It's not like we're in a relationship.

Maybe I should just leave?

But then his eyes lock onto mine, and my feet feel as if they're weighted in cement.

# Chapter 7
## Derek

"OKAY, Jenna. I'll make sure I call," I promise as my spine tingles. I swear I can feel Tessa before I see her, so I eagerly scope the crowd to see if she's returned.

I'm happy to find she's just a few feet away. Though instead of the playful expression I've come to expect, her brows are lowered, and her teeth bite into her lower lip.

Reaching for her hand, I pull her suddenly stiff body into my conversation with Jenna. "Hey, Tessa, this is Jenna. It's such a small world. She's here for her sister's bachelorette party this weekend."

"Congratulations." Tessa smiles. "Do you live around here?"

I haven't seen her around, but then again, I don't get out much.

Jenna laughs, and it's clear she's been drinking all day. "Nope—Matt and I live in Seattle now. We met Derek at U-Dub our freshman year when Matt was this guy's neighbor in the dorms." She thumbs in my direction, and I laugh at the memory.

Turning to Tessa, I explain, "I'll never forget when Matt got locked out of his dorm room in nothing but his boxers because Jenna left pissed, and he'd chased after her. I'd seen him around a few times, but we'd never spoken. I took pity on him and let him use the phone in my dorm while he waited for someone to unlock his door. We've been friends ever since— though we'd lost track of each other when I moved to Tacoma after graduation."

The more I explain, the more I see Tessa visibly relax, and her unreadable face becomes welcoming. Maybe I was just imagining her stiffness to begin with?

"Now that we all live in Seattle, we *have* to rectify that!"

"I'm here in Bear Creek for the next few months, but I won't be a stranger when I return," I quickly promise as the lead singer makes his way to the stage.

Jenna glances at the stage, then reaches in for a hug. "I gotta get back to my sister and the bridal party. It was great to see you, Derek. Don't be a stranger. Then she turns to Tessa. "It was nice meeting you."

Tessa barely gets a word in before Jenna bolts to the group of girls about ten feet in front of us. They each have a drink in hand and are swaying to the music playing in the background as we wait for the next headliner.

The next thing I know, the announcer introduces The Whiskey Barrels, and the place erupts with screams, whistles, and deafening noise. The energy radiating through the crowd is almost palpable.

Tessa's just as eager for the music as she turns her attention to the stage and screams right along with everyone else. When the lead singer makes his appearance, she quickly holds up her phone. I watch her snap a few photos, then quickly send it in a text to someone with a huge smile on her face.

"My dad will love this," she says as she leans in to be heard above the crowed. The smell of her intoxicating perfume makes my need for her grow. Giving in to the impulse, I pull her closer to slant my lips over hers. She closes the distance the second she realizes my intentions. When she darts her tongue out and meets mine, I nearly forget everyone in the stadium.

God, she tastes amazing. I'm taken off guard when she pulls back, but at the last second, she captures my lower lip between her teeth. That little tug alone has me wanting to leave now and have my way with her.

In our short time together, I've made her come countless times, but I have yet to experience the sensation of sinking into her. I fucking love learning her body. She's so responsive and entirely addictive. The next time I come, I need to be balls deep inside her.

Not wanting to miss the concert, she eventually ends our kiss and focuses her attention on the stage. Needing to continue our contact, I step close behind her, snaking my arms around her waist, and sway with her in rhythm to the music.

Her scent and the way her ass grinds against my dick does nothing to calm me down. Even though she feels amazing, I adjust us, giving myself some mercy. I may be a grown man, but she makes me feel like a teenager dry humping at a school dance. God, I can't wait to get her home.

Through the entire concert, I find myself touching her in one form or another. Eventually, I manage to focus on the band, but Tessa's never far from my mind. She knows almost every song and sings along with Hardy West, the lead singer. I only recognize their most popular songs by heart, so I'm impressed. It doesn't hurt that she has an amazing voice either.

By the time we return to my Range Rover, my ears are ringing. Tessa's must be, too, as we both amplify our voices to hear one another. Her voice is fucking sensual as hell as it's become raspy from singing and talking over the bands all day. It's a cross between Scarlett Johansson and Emma Stone, and the more she talks, the more I'm turned on. Both actresses were on my list of teenage crushes—but honestly, they have nothing on how sexy Tessa sounds in this moment.

"I wish my dad could've seen our favorite band," she says, reaching for my hand between the console. "Next time they're around, I'll have to get tickets for him."

"Is it tricky to plan around your dad's schedule?"

From the corner of my eye, I see Tessa shake her head. "If I give him enough notice, it won't be difficult."

As I pull into my parking spot, my chest tightens. Even though we've spent the entire day together, I'm not quite ready for my time with her to end. "I picked up some white chocolate strawberry rhubarb cookies, if you're interested."

Tessa eyes me suspiciously. "Are they from Honey Pots?"

I raise an eyebrow in challenge. "What do you think?"

I can bake—very simple things, but nothing like the drool-worthy concoctions they come up with. Ever since she introduced me to her favorite bakery earlier this week, I've eaten more pastries than I have in years.

Punching her hands to her hips, Tessa whips her head to me. "I think you've been holding out on me if you've had those in your apartment all day. You know those are like kryptonite to me, and I'll never turn them down."

Instead of answering, I just quirk a brow and smirk as I open the door.

Getting out of my vehicle, I walk around to meet Tessa. Though my mouth waters at the thought of tasting those treats, I'd rather taste her.

Reaching for Tessa's hand, I quickly brush my lips against hers before we ascend the stairs to my apartment. Once inside, all thoughts of the cookies fly right out the window when Tessa turns and plants a consuming kiss on my lips, the moment the door clicks shut.

"Miss me?" I tease between kisses. "I've been here all day."

"I know..." Kiss. "And it's..." Another kiss. "Been torture..."

"For you and me both, Tess," I admit as her hand snakes under the hem of my shirt.

The minute her fingers trace my abs, my cock strains, fighting for her attention.

The cargo shorts I'm wearing leave me no room to hide just how much her kisses affect me. "Fuck, you feel amazing," I growl as I unzip her hoodie to get better access to her beautiful body.

Tessa pushes up my shirt, and I step back, breaking our contact to pull it over my head, while she rids herself of her own shirt. When she steps back, she hesitates, which catches my full attention.

"What is it, Tessa?"

"Do you have condoms?"

"Condoms? As in more than one?" I playfully tease.

"Yes. I'm not sure once will be enough with you tonight."

I swear. This woman is made for me. "I bought an entire box. Is that enough?"

Her brows knit as she playfully pretends to contemplate. "It sounds like we've got our work cut out for us."

We may not have actually had sex yet, but I know in every fiber of my being by the tone of her voice and the way her eyes darken, she means every word. She's the most responsive woman I've met, and the challenging look in her eye tells me she's more than ready to take things to the next level.

"Bedroom?" she asks, feigning innocence. The moment I nod, she flicks the button of her shorts. Then she takes a few steps and unclasps her bra. As much as I want to be the one doing that to her, I'll admit it's hot as fuck seeing her in seductive mode.

"Two can play that game," I challenge, dropping my shorts to the floor with my boxers in tow.

When my cock springs to attention, and I'm standing here in all my naked glory, Tessa's tongue slowly licks her lower lip, and it's all I can do not to ravage her right here in my living room. Instead of walking toward me, she shimmies out of her shorts, pulling her underwear along with them. Once they're pooled into a pile on my floor, she smiles devilishly, then sprints in the opposite direction. "First one there's on top... at least for round one."

If she wants to be on top, who am I to complain? I can already picture her tear-shaped breasts hanging lusciously in front of my face as my fingertips play with one side, while my tongue ravages the other.

The moment I enter my room, my eyes land on hers. She's standing at the edge of the bed, giving me the come-hither motion with the crook of her finger. Her deep-blue eyes are filled with the perfect combination of lust and need. I'm not sure how it's possible, but the sensuality of her expression makes my cock even harder than before.

In a sexy as fuck voice, she rasps out, "Come here, you."

Yeah. I'd follow that voice anywhere.

Following her wishes, I lean in and slide my tongue along her collarbone to the pulse point on her neck that drives her wild. When her breath hitches, and she moans my name, I continue my assault on her body.

Fuck, she feels amazing.

Her hands reach for my cock and stroke it as I scrape my teeth along the rim of her ear as I whisper, "You've got me here, Tess. What are ya gonna do with me?"

"Hmmm... decisions... decisions," she whispers as she traces the head of my cock with her fingertips.

When she looks to her hands, I warn, "If you keep that up, this will be over before it starts."

A light chortle fills the room, and her sass shines. "Well, we wouldn't want that, would we? Hmmmm... let's see. I think it's time for you to lie back on the bed," she suggests, pressing a palm to my chest. Backing me against the bed with my calves.

Eagerly, I comply. I fall back and wriggle up the bed.

"Close your eyes."

Once the room turns dark, her fingers trace my inner leg up to my knee. Doing my best not to react, I sigh heavily in anticipation. When I feel the heat of her fingers at my thigh just millimeters from my balls, the bed dips.

"Fuck, Tessa," I groan as my dick bobs in greeting, hoping to be noticed.

I hear the smile on her lips as she says, "That's the plan... where did you say those condoms were?"

"In the nightstand drawer." I sound pitiful as she traces my length, then twirls her finger around the tip. "Oh... that feels... fucking incredible."

My eyes fly open as she leans forward, finding what she needs. Unfortunately, she has to stop her wicked torture to open the box. In a matter of moments, she's got a strip of condoms out and after removing one from the top, she throws them against the bed next to us.

Wanting to savor this moment, the words, "Come here, you," fly out of my mouth before I can stop them. Sure, I'd like nothing more than to fuck her into oblivion but as this is our first time, I need to make sure she's good and ready, begging for my cock by the time I enter her.

Needing her lips on mine, I pull her body up my torso, so I can kiss her once more. She falls to my side, and I roll to deepen our kiss.

*How is it possible she tastes even better than before?*

Letting my fingers roam, they trace down her spine, around her rib cage, and over her mound. When her legs fall apart to grant me better access, I tease her by slowly tracing her seam from her clit to her core as if I didn't have a care in the world.

"Derek…" she pants as her hips thrust into my hand with fervent need.

"Yes, beautiful?" I innocently ask, sliding one finger deep inside her.

"Ahhhh…" Her words are forgotten as I deepen our kiss, just as my thumb rubs circles around her clit. The moment I add a second finger inside her, her hips buck faster.

"Need… more…"

Her raspy voice has my dick turning to steel as it presses against her thigh.

"You've got me," I remind her, slipping in a third finger as I slowly pump in and out of her. As I feel her inner walls tighten, I break our kiss and pluck a luscious nipple between my teeth. Her orgasm erupts like wildfire, spreading from her core to her outer extremities.

I feel like I'm king of the world as she trembles and quakes, riding out every last wave of ecstasy. I've done this. I've made her feel this way, and I have every intention of doing it over and over throughout the rest of the night.

But of course, Tessa has other plans.

As soon as she catches her breath, she lifts her head and grins wickedly. "While I have zero complaints about what you just did, I won fair and square when I raced you to the bedroom. It's my turn to have my way with you, Derek."

Fuck, she's gorgeous when she's determined.

Of course, my dick takes notice and stands at full attention, at the mere mention of her words. Fuck. I don't think I've ever been harder than I am looking at Tessa.

Before I know it, she's grabbing a condom and straddling my thighs. In seconds, she rips the foil wrapper open. It only takes her a moment to roll the condom over my length and have us protected. Needing to taste her, I pull her lips to mine and get my fill. I'm not sure I I'll ever get enough of those luscious lips.

Damn, she tastes amazing. The perfect combination between sweet and sin. A mix of mint and all things Tessa. Wanting to make sure she's ready, I reach between her thighs and stroke her.

"Oh, Derek," she says between kisses. "I need you inside me. I can't wait any more."

Me neither. I need her more than I need my next breath.

"I'm right here, Tess..." I kiss her once more as she takes my cock in her hand and aligns me with her entrance. Resting her hand on my chest, she lowers herself just enough to take part of me in. I hiss in appreciation. For our first time, I want to savor this moment.

She pulls back, then works her way down my length, again and again, until our pelvic bones meet. The moment she's fully seated on me, she moans with satisfaction. "This is so much better than I imagined."

Placing her other hand on the headboard, she leans forward, and I pull one of her perfect breasts into my mouth. Swirling my tongue around her hard nipple, I smile in satisfaction. Fuck, she always tastes amazing. "For you and me both, Tess," I admit.

Tilting her hips, she rocks forward, and I find myself thrusting deeper inside her. Fuck, the way she sways her hips at the end, right before she slams back down on me, feels fucking insane. I barely notice her hand leave my chest to steady herself against my headboard, as our rhythm increases. Thrust for thrust, she meets me with an intensity I've never experienced.

When the pricks of electricity spark in my spine, I know I need to bring her with me. Pressing my thumb against her clit, I apply the perfect amount of pressure to drive her wild.

"Oh, God, Derek," she pants. "Right there."

"Let go, Tess," I practically beg. "Let me feel you come again..."

My body hurdles toward a cliff, and I fight like hell to hold on until she can tumble over the edge with me. When her inner muscles clench around my cock, I swivel my hips from beneath, to intensify our connection.

The next thing I know, Tessa's coming apart. Pulse after pulse, wave after wave, I jump off the ledge with her, reveling in the ecstasy. As soon as her body stops quaking above me, she collapses onto my chest. "God," I pant between breaths as I trace her spine. "I seriously never wanted that to end."

Her voice is muffled from my chest as she says, "Me neither."

As our breathing returns to normal, I trace circles along the tattoos covering the top of her arm. I feel her body shift to reach over to the box of tissues I have on the bedside table and rid me of the condom. Lazily, she drapes herself over me once I'm settled.

Absentmindedly, I continue tracing the shapes of her

tattoo. Needing to know more about her, I ask, "How old were you when you got your first tattoo?"

Pulling her head off my chest to look at me, she points to the three roses just below the face of a clock, with its gears showing. "I got this just after high school graduation. These three roses represent those I lost. My mom's the biggest, then my grandma and grandpa." When she's finished, she rests her head back on my chest, and I wrap my arms around her.

I knew her tattoo would have meaning, but I wasn't expecting her to open up so quickly. In our short time together, I've learned that Tessa doesn't talk much about her loss. She focuses on the positive things she's been given.

"What about the two roses below?" I ask, tracing their outlines on her arm, when she settles her head back on my chest.

"Those are for my dad and me. The clock and the open lock on the chain remind me that we've only been given so much time on earth. My grandma always wore a locket around her neck and was big on making sure it wasn't a secret to know how much she loved me."

She takes a deep breath, then continues down an unexpected path.

"When I got old enough to realize I was the cause of my mother's death, I took it to heart. More than anything, my dad and grandma made it their mission in life to let me know I was loved. Even though she didn't know my mom for more than a few years, Grandma made sure I knew all there was to know about her. Heck, she even reached out to my mom's parents to create a photo album, especially for me. She pumped my mom's family full of questions, so she'd have so many stories to tell."

Tessa sighs at a memory as she absentmindedly traces patterns across my upper arm. "She told me story after story about how much my mom couldn't wait to meet me. She wanted me from the moment she found out she was pregnant. She knew she was young but was happily married and couldn't wait to start a family with my dad. She was convinced I was a girl long before they even knew for sure. She even had my name picked out within weeks of finding out about me."

Not wanting her to stop, I probe, "How old was she?"

"My mom was twenty-three when I was born. She'd been in labor with me for nearly fifteen hours when the doctors discovered my heart rate was low, and I was in fetal distress. Being the selfless woman she was, Mom begged the doctors to save me—no matter the cost. Especially when she found out her uterus had ruptured. The doctors did everything they could to save us both. At one point, they thought we were in the clear, but her bleeding wouldn't stop, and she didn't survive."

Fuck. My chest tightens, and my heart aches for Tessa.

Not having any words, I just squeeze her tighter.

"From what I've been told, Dad was a wreck for months. But he'd promised to be there for me, and he wouldn't go back on his word to my mom. Eventually, he pulled himself together and moved forward with life. My grandparents were supportive, so he never had to do it on his own."

I can't even imagine. I'd be fucking devastated if I lost the love of my life with a newborn baby.

She sucks in a deep breath. "But you only asked how old I was. It took many sessions to finish this tattoo."

She's quiet for a moment, then apologizes as she kisses my chest. "Sorry. Thanks for letting me have a moment... to answer your question, I was eighteen. I still get new ink every year or so. I guess you can say I'm addicted to ink and haven't stopped."

Again, I'm at a loss for words. Tessa has been through so much, and you'd never know it by just looking at her. On the outside, she's a fucking tank. She's strong, independent, and is the most put-together person I know.

She catches me off guard when she lifts her head to look me in her eye. "What about you?"

Not following her, I ask, "What about me?"

"Do you think you'll ever put some ink on this perfect body of yours?" She smirks as she bites my nipple playfully. Obviously, she's trying to lighten the mood, so I'll roll with it.

"My body is hardly perfect..." I scoff. Lifting her chin, I bend my head to kiss her. It's not as fervent as before, but just as sensual.

When we pull apart, she traces my pecs as she drawls out, "So...?"

Fuck. She asked me a question.

Think, Derek...

"I've always liked the idea of ink but haven't found anything I'd want on my body permanently, though I've had a few designs rolling around in my head."

"I'd love to see them... someday..." Her voice trails off.

"I'll make you a deal—When I finally decide, you'll be the first to know about it."

Her brows lift, and I hear disbelief in her voice when she faces me once more. "So you're getting one while you're here?"

Shit. That's not what I meant—but as I stare at her gorgeous ink—I'm certainly not opposed to it either. "If I find the right artist and finish the design I've been working on."

"Oh," Tessa says enthusiastically as she lifts on to her elbow for better eye contact. "I'll have to introduce you to mine. Dax is the best. I'm not sure he'll be able to get you in before you leave, but if he has any openings, I'd highly advise you to not pass it up."

For the first time since arriving, the fact that my time here in Colorado has an expiration date hits me. My chest tightens, and an uneasy feeling settles in the pit of my stomach. Somehow, I keep my tone steady when I nod. "If he can fit me in, I'll keep that in mind."

"You'd better," Tessa says as she pokes the center of my chest. "I think you'd look super sexy with some ink."

"Is tall and tatted your type?" I ask playfully. But the moment those words fall from my lips, images pop up from earlier of Jace and his inked arms wrapping around Tessa.

Fuck. Why did my mind have to go there?

Fuck. There it is again. Leaving.

"Speaking of leaving, and guys your type..." I trail off.

"What about it?" Tessa says, piercing me with electrifying blue eyes.

"I'm not ready for my time with you to end." The words fall from my lips before I can think about the repercussions.

"Well, that's good," she says as she brushes a kiss against my lips. "I'm not ready for that either. This was only our first time, and I'm pretty sure there's a few more things I'd like to do with you." Her tone turns suggestive at the end, making my cock twitch and want attention.

"I'm not a guy who likes to share," I admit.

Warily, her eyes focus on mine. "Uh... Derek, I don't really do long-term relationships. I barely have time for me, let alone a serious commitment."

The last week with her flows through my mind. There's no way I'm ready to walk away from this just yet—especially if I'm here until October. Needing to kiss her, I slowly pull her body up mine as a brilliant compromise comes to mind. "It's a good thing—because I'm only here for a couple of months. We both just admitted we're not ready for our time together to end... And since I'm not one to share... What do you say? Wanna keep this thing we've got going between us exclusive?"

Not waiting for an answer, my lips crash onto her soft lips. When she darts her tongue out to meet mine, I roll our bodies so that I'm on top. Eventually, I realize I need an answer to my question, so I pull away breathless and wait for her eyes to lock on mine.

"Do we have ourselves a deal?" I ask, nipping at her lips once more. She tastes incredible, and all I want in this moment is more.

Tessa's grin is wide as she rolls her eyes. "I think I can

handle that. Especially if you do that thing you did so well the other night when I was here."

Knowing she could be talking about a number of things, I playfully smile. "You'll have to refresh my memory."

Instead of answering, Tessa reaches out, snaking her arms around my neck, and tugs me closer. "Right now, I just want your lips on mine."

# Chapter 8
## Tessa

"NITA, WHAT WAS I THINKING?" I practically whine into the phone as I walk into my dad's kitchen. He's picked up an unexpected shift and has asked me to empty his fridge of perishables, so there won't be any science experiments when he returns.

"Uh, you were thinking you're in bed with a hot guy and you want to fuck his brains out?" Nita points out the obvious.

"Nita..." I draw out. "You're not helping."

Her loud laugh comes through the phone. "What? If you don't want him, maybe give a girl a break and hook us up. I need someone who gives me multiples with just the flick of a tongue."

"God. Why did I tell you that?" I say more to myself than her. I love my best friend, but why is she pushing me so hard on this? She knows me. She knows what I'm capable of when it comes to relationships. More importantly, what I'm not.

"Relax, T. I'd never go after your man."

"He's not my man," I quickly spit out, though the denial sounds weak, even to my ears.

"Uh... I'm pretty sure he is," Nita reminds me.

"Gah.... I think I was under a euphoric trance or something. Is orgasmic bliss a thing? Why else would I commit to being with him exclusively?"

Nita's silent for a moment, but when she speaks, all traces of humor are gone. "Tess, are you serious?"

"Yes... I mean..." Fuck. What do I mean? "No. You know me, I'm a serial monogamist. I don't sleep with more than one person at a time—but I also don't do commitments. I barely have time for myself and every spare moment I have is spent at Bed Knobs."

"Tessa," Nita sighs exasperatedly. "You yourself said Derek is only here for a few months. If things don't work out, they won't, and you won't be with him that long."

"I know," I draw out in defeat. "But I just don't do relationships."

"Has he given you any indication that you're not compatible? I mean, I know you're sizzling between the sheets, but do you connect with him when your clothes are on?"

"Are you slut-shaming me?" I tease, trying to miss her obvious point. I focus on the task at hand—cleaning out the fridge.

"Not at all, we all have our needs and to each thy own. But this is you. You told me you had a lot of fun at the concert... but can you live next door to Derek and have him bringing someone else home?"

Images of Jenna from the concert flash through my mind. There's no way I'd admit to Nita, how I was green with envy that she was hugging him—even if they were only friends from college.

"That's what I thought," Nita says in triumph.

"But..." I start, but my argument is stuck in my throat—because let's face it—I don't have one.

"Tess, Derek is ideal for the perfect fling. He works from home most days and can deal with your crazy schedule. You obviously have other things in common, or you wouldn't have spent the day with him at the music festival. I know you—you wouldn't waste your time on a dud. Besides, he's only here for a few months. What's the worse that happens?"

I could catch feelings.

Uggh... I can't go there. I don't do relationships.

Knowing she meant her question as rhetorical, I Ignore it. "Did I tell you I'm taking Derek to the archery range this afternoon?"

"Uh... no, you didn't. You never take guys to the range—that's something you and Gramps did."

Ignoring her statement, I quickly explain, "He's extremely competitive. Since I smoked him on our fishing trip, he challenged me on the range when I brought up things I like to do for fun."

Nita's silent, so I blurt out, "I kinda feel sorry for him... because I may not have mentioned that I used to shoot competitively."

"Holy shit, T. That's just mean. That poor guy doesn't stand a chance."

"Uh... considering he's never been to a range before, probably not."

"Is he at least a good loser?"

"Well, I got my fish cleaned, an amazing dinner, and multiple O's out of our last deal. What do you think?"

"I think I need to find a man like Derek," Nita sighs. "You said he has brothers, right? Any chance they could be coming for a visit?"

"Sorry, Nita. His brother Damien just got engaged, and his brother Davis is too busy in med school. Besides, he lives in Portland, and that would be geographically undesirable, don't ya think?"

"A girl can dream, right?" Nita sighs.

"Sometimes Derek is too good to be true," I say before I can stop myself.

"Hmmmm..." Nita draws out. She doesn't have to say anything. I know she's thinking about me catching feelings for Derek. And I guess I am—if you count wanting to chase the constant orgasmic high he likes to keep me in.

There's a muffled noise from the background, and Nita says something to someone in the room. "Listen, I've gotta run. I promised Shane I'd take him shopping for some new clothes. Apparently now that you've given him a steady gig, he wants more than three pairs of jeans."

I've always loved Nita's relationship with her brother Shane. "Tell him I can't wait to see him perform next Thursday. Love you, Nita. I'll be at the archery range this afternoon, then I'm working tonight. I'll catch up with you tomorrow."

"Promise you'll go easy on the guy, T. Not all of us are regional champs. God, I sure hope the guy can at least hit the broad side of a barn, or you'll never make it through September."

"Ha. Ha," I snark. "He's man enough to accept defeat when it happens."

"Good... Shane's giving me the death stare. So, I'll catch ya later. I'm looking forward to meeting this infamous Derek."

Before I can respond, the line goes dead. Leave it to Nita to always have the last word.

It doesn't take me long to finish cleaning out the fridge and to water a few of the plants we've managed to keep alive since Grandma passed. I'd grabbed the mail on my way in, so it's already on the table, waiting for Dad when he returns. Thankfully, I convinced him to go paperless with most of our bills, so he doesn't get much mail to begin with.

It doesn't take long before I'm in my car, heading back to town. As the miles get closer, my mind drifts to Derek. I still can't believe he got me to agree to his antics, but one thing is certain—I'm not ready for my time with him to end.

---

"FINALLY!" Derek shouts when he hits his first bullseye. I let him warm up for a bit after teaching him the ropes. He's one of the sexiest men alive when it comes to giving a task that requires his entire focus. The way his black tee stretches across his back as he lines up his shot, nearly has me losing my ability to focus on anything else. In fact, I even made some major errors because I'd been watching him and not lining up my aim for the target.

The indoor target range I like to practice in is empty as it's barely after noon on a Tuesday. One nice thing about Derek's flexible schedule is we can find time to spend together around my commitments. Between brewing in the specialty blends out on my family's property and covering shifts at Bed Knobs, I never know when I'll get a free moment. Thankfully, Derek doesn't seem to mind.

I find myself watching him unload all his arrows into the target, instead of focusing on my own. With each round, he is improving, but he still has yet to get another arrow to land in the center ring. When he glances over his shoulder between shots and catches me staring, he impishly grins. "Am I doing something wrong?"

"No, not at all," I quickly assure him. Though let's be honest, my eyes have been plastered on his backside and not his shooting form. Damn. The guy knows how to fill out a pair of jeans.

Quirking a brow, he asks, "Then why aren't you shooting?"

*Because your ass is a better target to set my sights on?*

"I'm just letting you get warmed up." I shrug, feigning innocence.

His eyes dance, and a smile plays at his lips as he challenges, "Step up to the line and take your best shot."

"Are you sure you want to go there?"

"What's good for the goose, is good for the gander." He smirks. "If you're gonna stare at my ass all day, it's only fair I get to do the same." He slowly shrugs with a wink as he tacks on, "Equal rights and all."

"Cocky much?" I smirk. "What makes you think I'm staring at your ass?"

His sexy laugh fills the room. "Well, the way your eyes bugged out when I mentioned it was my first clue. Besides, that expression on your face is priceless."

Unwilling to acknowledge the truth in his statement, I step up to the line and set my stance, making sure I wiggle my ass in his direction before taking it seriously. Continuing my show, I pretend to adjust my arm guard, then I extend my arm that's grasping the handle. Slowly, I draw back my string until I anchor it against my right cheek. Taking a second to adjust my aim, I release the string, and my arrow zooms to my intended target, landing smack dab in the center bullseye.

From the corner of my eye, I see Derek shake his head. "Ah... so that's how it's gonna be. I was gonna make a friendly wager, but seeing as I'd likely have my ass handed to me, I'd rather bet on your talents."

Lowering my bow, I cockily challenge, "And what would that entail?"

"If you can lump the rest of your arrows in that center circle, you get to decide where I should put my first piece of ink on my body. Your buddy Dax called this morning and said he had a cancellation in a couple of weeks."

"Well, that seems simple enough." I shrug. Then another thought hits. "But what if I miss?" Surely, it can't be that bad.

"You let me design your next ink—and before you say anything—I promise it'll match your style."

Derek's fucking brilliant when it comes to design. This is a win-win for me. So of course, I take the bet. Without saying a word, I nod once as I step up to the line and cluster my next three shots around the first. This is as easy as taking candy from a baby.

Just as I'm about to take my last shot, my cockiness gets the best of me, and I glance his way. His arms are crossed over his broad chest, and a knowing smile plays at his lips. When I hesitate, he cocks a brow as if to say, *well, what are you waiting for*.

Refocusing my attention on the target, I slowly exhale before extending my arm. With careful precision, I draw back until my anchor is set. I wait until I exhale once more before releasing the arrow.

I swear, I hear Derek gasp as he waits for the verdict.

Knowing what's done is done, I close my eyes and wait for Derek's response to tell me if I've won or not. This was truly one of those cases where I'll come out ahead either way, but waiting those few seconds feels as if time has stood still.

When Derek whoops loudly, I turn and focus my attention to him. His long strides close the distance between us and the next thing I know, I'm being swooped into his arms. "You're a freaking goddess."

With the bow still in hand, he spins me around.

"Put me down, you Neanderthal," I say through broken laughter.

Instead of putting me directly on my feet, Derek slowly lets my body slide along his until only my toes reach the cement below us. When our lips align, he holds me in place as his mouth slants over mine.

The warmth of his breath and the scent of his cologne makes my belly flip in anticipation. Reaching my free hand behind his neck, I pull him closer, and his lips crash onto mine. If kissing was an Olympic sport, Derek would always win gold. He's found the way to keep things light, yet makes me want to undress him with just a single kiss. Hell, I can barely remember my name when he darts his tongue out to play with mine.

Eventually, a noise from outside the range reminds me that we're in public. He must have heard it, too, as our kiss slows, and we eventually part. Running his thumb along my now-swollen lips, he smiles. "I can't wait to see where you think my tattoo should go."

Is it weird that I almost wish I hadn't won? The thought of his art on me, reminding me of this very moment, would've almost been worth it. Even when he's gone, I want to remember how free and cherished I feel.

Before I can say anything stupid, I quickly ask, "Do you already have the design made?"

"Yeah, I started working on one about a year ago. I still want to make a few final tweaks, but I'm close."

"If you had the design, I'm sure there were artists in Seattle. Why now?"

"I love Dax's work." He runs a finger down my arm, admiring his work.

But is he ready for something permanent? That was one of his reasons before.

I certainly don't want him only getting ink based on a bet.

One that I wasn't honest about either.

Fuck. I need to come clean. This wasn't a fair bet.

"Uh..." I bite into my lower lip, wondering how I should tell him.

May as well rip off the Band-Aid. I could never live with myself if I weren't straight with him. "Did I ever mention..." I almost chicken out. But I steel my back and look him in the eyes as I spit out, "I used to be a competitive archer?"

Derek's perfect jaw drops, then clamps tight for a few moments before a devilish smirk forms. "I don't believe you've mentioned that, no. Anything else you've got up your sleeve? Are you a pool shark? Do you count cards? Maybe you're a secret ninja spy?"

Swatting at his chest, I say, "Don't be ridiculous. A ninja spy? Really? What on earth would make you think that? I'm nowhere near stealthy. Trust me."

"Okay, so I should never play pool against you or take you to Vegas. Got it. Wait! Are you even allowed in Vegas?" His face is so expressive, it's hard to tell if he's joking or being serious.

Punching my fists into my hips, I play along. "For your information... I suck at pool. And as for counting cards, I wouldn't have the first clue how. I've never been a gambler, so I've never played."

"You've enjoyed kicking my ass, so what's next? I'm pretty competitive, but I want a fair shake. You never told me you were the fish whisperer, and you just proved you're a shark with archery."

Poking him in his chest to prove my point, I quickly add, "I'm not a shark. You're the one who made that bet, *after* you saw me get that bullseye. If anything, I'd say you were dying to lose, so you couldn't back out of getting that tattoo you've always wanted."

"Hey, hey, hey," he says, grabbing my index finger and snaking his free arm around my hip to pull me closer. "The moment you took that first shot, I knew you wouldn't agree to a game you couldn't lose."

His eyes bore into mine as if he's willing me to give up.

"But..." I start because I'm that stubborn, but he stops me with his finger pressing against my lips.

"Tessa, I'd never do anything I don't want to do. If I was willing to take you up on another bet..." He freaking winks at me mischievously. "I'm guessing you won't either."

"You can bet your ass I won't," I say before I can stop myself.

"There will be no betting on my ass... especially when it comes to you, *Miss I can't lose at anything*. I happen to love my ass and from the way you were looking at it earlier, you do, too."

Ohmigod! I can't even—with this man.

# Chapter 9
## Derek

NOT EVEN TWO minutes after Tessa leaves for work, my phone rings. Figuring she must have left something at my place, I swipe to answer my phone and ask, "Forget something?"

"Not that I can think of," a much deeper voice than I'm expecting says. It most definitely isn't the sexy brunette who just rocked my world before heading off to work. Nope. It's Damien, my brother.

"Hey, Dame, what's up?" I say as I plop down on the couch to get comfortable.

"Who'd you think forgot something?" I can tell by the tone in his voice, he's smirking, and his brow is quirked. I'd bet my last paycheck, he also knows I'm talking about a girl.

No sense in lying.

"Tessa."

"Hmmm..." Dame draws out as if he's waiting for more. But I'm not ready to talk about her yet. Especially with my family. If Mom or Dani catch wind of me hanging out with a girl, they'll have me married off in no time.

Damien breaks the silence. "Okay... I see that's how you're gonna play this. You'll let me know if you ever get serious about a woman, won't you?"

"Not everyone proposes within months of meeting some-one, Dame," I tease my younger brother. I'm so happy for him and Vanessa, but even he'll admit he hasn't known her long. Though when I saw them together at my sister's wedding, they looked even more in love than Dani and Luke. I didn't think that was even possible.

"Speaking of engagements... Van and I set a date for the wedding."

"Really? When's that?" I ask in disbelief. They just got engaged a few weeks ago, and I'm certain weddings take time to plan.

"August seventh."

"Of next year?" He can't be talking about next month, can he?

There's a long pause. "I know you just got to Bear Creek, but I'm referring to this August."

Holy shit. He can't be serious. This has to be one of the shortest engagements in history. "What's the rush?" I ask, more accusatory than I intend. *Is she pregnant or something?*

Damien's deep laugh echoes through the phone. "When you know, you know, man. But seriously. She's it for me. With everything that happened to her parents, neither of us wants to waste a minute being apart. Besides, with Jules, we need consistency."

Jules may only be five years old, but she stole the hearts of my entire family when we met her earlier this month.

"I can see that," I admit. "But..."

"But I'm a selfish bastard. I want to sleep next to Vanessa every night. It doesn't make sense for me to move in with

Vanessa, her brother, Jules, *and* his fiancée when I have a perfectly good house of my own, a few miles away."

"True..." I start, but he cuts me off again.

"Vanessa and Jules start school in September. We just want to get things settled before then."

"Look, man, you don't have to convince me. I know you love her. It was evident to anyone in the room at Dani's wedding. I'm just surprised the wedding's in mere weeks. I guess when you set your mind to something, there's no holding back."

"Ha, you know me. Dani cannot outdo me."

Groaning at Dani's surprise wedding, I admit, "Thanks for not making it a surprise. I was so pissed she made us all show up and then went AWOL."

"Will it be a problem for you to fly in for the weekend?"

"With such short notice," I point out. "Where's the wedding anyway?" Pulling out my laptop, I pull up my favorite search engine to get a decent flight, wondering if I should fly into Seattle or Portland.

"Vanessa insists on getting married in my backyard. I haven't finished landscaping, but now you know what I'll be working on every spare second I have, until the day arrives. Honestly, I might just hire it out so neither of us will stress about it."

Portland it is.

"What can I do to help?" I offer, feeling guilty for being in Colorado when he could use some manual labor. Davis lives close by, but he's in med school, and who knows what his schedule's like with his current rotation.

"Uh, showing up is more than enough." It's almost as if the thought of me helping is absurd. I'm not having it.

"Seriously, Dame, I may be thousands of miles away, but I'd like to help. Let me at least look into a landscaper for you. You can consider *that* my gift for the wedding."

"You may be my *older* brother, but I'm perfectly capable of handling this. Besides, I did a lot before inviting everyone over for the proposal. There won't be too much more to do."

"Seriously, at least let me do something. Dani didn't let us do a thing."

"Well... you could be my best man?" he asks.

"Seriously?" This is such an honor. Between Davis and me, I thought for sure Dame would choose a close friend or something, so he wouldn't be forced to choose.

"Don't get your ego inflated." Damien chuckles, then admits, "I flipped a coin between you and Davis. Vince will also be a groomsman after he gives Van away... Margo, Sydney, and Dani will be Van's bridesmaids and of course, Jules will be the flower girl."

"Do I need a tux?"

"Just a black suit is fine. Vanessa's picking out ties—so just a white shirt will work."

"Have you told the Rents yet? I'll bet Mom's over the moon."

"I'm surprised you couldn't hear her screams from there."

"Nope, no screaming here," I tease. "But I can only imagine."

My parents fell in love with Jules, and her mom Vanessa, at Dani's wedding. With the way Dad danced with Jules all night, you'd think he grew ten years younger in the short time he spent with her.

"Listen, I need to call Dani and Davy. Are you good with making travel arrangements? We live so close to the airport, we'll pick you up, and you can plan on staying with me. Mom and Dad insist on renting a hotel so Grandma and Pops can stay with them. We're keeping it a relatively small wedding. If you can arrive Thursday, Davis is insisting on throwing a bachelor party."

Suddenly, a thought hits me. "Were you able to get a minister in that short of time?"

"Oh, brother, you wouldn't believe what a whirlwind it's been around here. Would you believe my buddy Jack from the diner has been an ordained minister for years? I swear that guy lives up to his name. He's a Jack of all trades, or so he claims."

"I can't wait to meet him." From my understanding, that guy kept Dame on his toes when he first met Vanessa. "And look at you—you're already making dad jokes."

"Don't get me wrong, I love the hell out of Van, but I fell just as hard for Jules. I'm nervous about being a dad, but after she gave me the what-for before Dani's wedding, I'm sure I'm ready for it."

"Hey, the girl knows what she wants." I still can't believe that sweet girl sat my brother down and asked him to be her dad. I would've been shitting bricks, but Dame handled everything like a pro.

Dame's unusually quiet for longer than necessary. "What's going on, Dame?"

"Did I tell you I'm adopting Julia?"

"What? When did this happen?" Holy shit—when he said whirlwind, he wasn't kidding.

I swear, I just saw him a few weeks ago, and none of this had happened. Of course, I couldn't be at his actual proposal because I'd just gotten here, but Davis told me it was epic. Vanessa didn't have a clue it was coming, and Jules being Jules stole the show.

"Vanessa and I have been talking. Even though Julia's biological dad will eventually be in the picture in some form or another, we've decided it's important she and Vanessa have the same last name. Besides—from the moment we got engaged, Jules asked if she'd be a Fallon, too. Leave it to her to set things in motion."

"Holy shit, man, that's huge. I'm so glad everything's falling into place for you. You totally deserve it."

"Thanks, D. Listen, I gotta run. Text me your details, and I'll pick you up."

"Will do. Love ya, Dame."

"Love you more. Thanks for being my best man."

"Always."

Hanging up the phone, I stare at the wall as I process the bombs Damien just dropped. My brother's getting married—next month. He's adopting Julia, and everything he's ever wished for has fallen into place. I just have one question as thoughts of Tessa roll through my mind—how the hell did he know *Vanessa was the one*, so fast?

# Chapter 10

## Tessa

WAKING up to an empty bed is something I should be used to, but since I agreed to being exclusive with Derek, I'm not. My sheets still smell like him, as he only left yesterday to attend his brother's wedding. Rolling over, I snuggle the pillow he'd been using and slowly inhale. God, it smells amazing.

It's times like this that I truly think adulting sucks.

Sure, he'd asked me to fly to Portland with him, but I couldn't. This is the only weekend the entire summer that we've double-booked our events. I've committed to covering a wedding for Bed Knobs & Brews, while Marek is covering a festival in Aspen. Marek shies away from scheduling formal events, but the money this family is offering to pay is something I just can't turn down. Besides, they're regular customers, and I don't want to disappoint them.

Between covering some shifts at the brewery for Kylie, who's also requested this week off, doing the wedding event, and visiting my dad on Sunday, it's not like I would've seen much of Derek anyway. It's probably best he's out of town.

The poor guy has been busting his ass to finish some designs for his client so he can walk away today and not think about work for an entire week. Derek returns Monday afternoon, but Tuesday is his appointment with Dax.

From what he's shown me about his design, he'll be spending most of the day in Dax's chair when he returns. The only place his tattoo makes sense to be is on either his left or right shoulder. Selfishly, since I typically sleep on his right side, I've suggested the quarter sleeve tat be on his left shoulder. I know he's leaving, and that won't matter in the long term, but I want to enjoy every moment of time with him I can before his impending departure.

With Shane and his band performing tonight, I'm sure I'll be working well past two in the morning. Just as I expected, they're starting to draw in their own crowd of followers. They each have one more year left in college, but I'm sure if they keep this up, their college degrees will merely be something to fall back on.

Tossing back the covers, I reluctantly stumble to the shower to start my day. I'd much rather snuggle in bed and remember my night with Derek, but my to-do list won't complete itself. If I'm lucky, it will remain uneventful, and the weekend will fly by.

---

BY SATURDAY AFTERNOON, things are still going smooth. I've covered Kylie's shift at the brewery, then made it home with plenty of time to change into my favorite little black dress to show I've made an effort for the wedding. Since this isn't our first rodeo with formal events, Nita and I even bought matching dresses we jokingly call our formal work uniforms for weddings and fancier occasions.

Since I only do a few of these a year, Nita insists on helping with these events. It's something that started out as her helping me out in a pinch and turned into our thing. She claims she never has a reason to dress up and spend time with her bestie. Personally, I think we'd have more fun just hanging out at her house or mine, but if this is what makes her happy, who am I to refuse her help?

I had a crew set up for the wedding earlier in the day, so Nita and I essentially only have to show up, work the event, and the crew will return tomorrow to pick up what's left. As much as I tease Nita, I couldn't do these without her. She's saved my ass so many times since starting out on my own. Unfortunately, she's completely content with her day job as the director of our local youth center, so I couldn't convince her to work with me permanently.

When I pull up to Nita's, she's already outside her house. I barely get the chance to stop before she opens the door. As soon as she hops in and slams the door, she exhales heavily.

Checking for cars, I return to the roadway. "In a hurry much? What am I? Your driveaway car?"

"Sort of," she sighs. "My brother has a few of his friends over to listen to their latest song, and one just won't stop hitting on me."

When Nita's parents decided to retire and drive around the country in their RV, she bought their family home. The only catch is that Shane and his band members are there most days each summer, while he's in college.

"He probably couldn't help it if he saw you in that dress. You're hot."

"Ugh, but he's so much younger than me."

"Aren't most of Shane's friends legal to drink? I've seen most of them in the bar. I'd know if they had fake IDs." If not, I'm gonna kick his ass, personally.

"Yes, they're all over twenty-one. But it's weird."

"It's not like four to five years older makes you a cougar or anything."

From the corner of my eye, I see her scrunch up her nose. "But still... I used to babysit some of those guys."

"But not when they were actually babies. Five years is not that big of a deal. Besides, you're always saying that you're ready to start dating again."

"Not *any* of my brother's friends!" she yells. "That's just wrong on so many levels."

"If you say so. Some are just three years younger," I point out, then a thought hits me, "Wait, are you saying you won't date a guy five years older then?"

"I'm not opposed to it." She shrugs.

"I love you, Nita, but that's such a double standard. If you can date someone five years older, why won't you date someone five years younger? We're only twenty-six. It seems crazy when you think about it."

She looks out the window and doesn't say anything for a while.

"Can you at least tell me his name, so I can see if he's worthy for you myself?"

Nita snickers before mumbling, "It's Jake."

"Seriously?" I ask in disbelief. "What's wrong with him? He's going to school to become an electrical engineer, so he's got a good head on his shoulders. Let's get real..." I draw out for emphasis. "He's freaking Italian—as in he was born in Rome. What am I missing? Last I checked, tall, dark, and handsome were kinda everyone's type."

"I don't know. I've just programmed myself not to look at Shane's friends that way," she admits. "Speaking of tall, dark, and handsome, what's going on between you and your upstairs neighbor?"

My body reacts before my mind can stop my lips from curling into a smile. "Derek and I are still seeing each other—but it's not serious. He's leaving in October, and we're enjoying our time together." Before she can pry any further, I quickly turn the focus back to her. "And nice try—we're talking about you." Her lips purse, and her brows knit. "The look on your face tells me there's something more," I probe. Knowing each other for years means neither of us can get away with much. If she doesn't want to talk about it, I'll respect her privacy, but something tells me there's more to what she's revealing.

"It's nothing... really." Her teeth sink into her lower lip as she rubs her hands along her thigh.

Yeah, she's holding back.

Apparently, my silence is enough to push her further because she quietly admits, "We uh... sort of kissed this afternoon."

I know I shouldn't, but a laugh escapes. "How do you sort of kiss? Did he trip and fall, landing in your lips?"

"We were hanging out waiting for Shane and his band-mates to finish their practice... and well, one thing led to another."

"What's the bigger issue here? You like him, or is it that he's your brother's friend?"

I pull into my parking spot just as Nita shrugs. "Both?"

"For what it's worth, I say go for it. Maybe have a conversation with Shane and see if he objects to it majorly. But if Jake makes you happy, I'm sure Shane will see that, too."

"But isn't it weird that I'm so much older than him?"

"You're not his grandmother's age, for crying out loud. You're less than five years older. Who cares?"

Once we get out of our vehicle, a member of the bride's family interrupts our conversation. "Hi, Tessa. I'm Dean. It's great to see you again. I've been tasked to show you around and get you anything else you might need."

Inside the reception hall, I'm delighted to see my employees have everything set up and ready for us to serve as soon as guests arrive. Dean also shows us around the venue, pointing out the restrooms and kitchen as we walk around. Once we're done with the tour, Nita and I go to work. We familiarize ourselves with what's in stock and arrange like we've done dozens of times, to ensure we're able to flow around one another.

When the reception starts, Nita and I have our work cut out for us. I knew the guest list was just over two hundred, but they all want a taste of my specialty brew. Sure, we're also serving hard alcohol and wine, but from the moment the reception started, there's a steady flow of people.

The line settles when dinner is served, and everyone has their beverage of choice. Just a few guests trickle up to the bar, so Nita and I use this reprieve to restock and reorganize. Nita takes out the trash, while I serve the stragglers.

When a man saunters up to the bar, I think nothing of it. With a friendly smile, I greet him. "Hi! What can I get for you?"

Unlike the usual guest who quickly rattle off their drink order, this guy stops and leans against the bar. I can tell from the tux, he's a groomsman. Before he says anything, the room erupts with noise, and our attention is drawn to the bride and groom who've done something I've evidently missed.

When everything's calmed down, the groomsman's blue eyes roam over my tattoos and back to my face before he glances over to our list of specialty brews we have on hand.

While he reads, I do what I do best. I people watch. You can tell a lot about a person, from their stance to the way they carry themselves. I'll admit he's not hard on the eyes. He runs a hand through his blond hair, then turns his attention to me.

He's not my type, but I can appreciate the view all the same.

No, my type is attending a different wedding at the moment. But I'm not dead yet either.

"Can I get a Slumbering Bear? That's one of your darkest beers, right?"

"Sure thing." I quickly tilt a glass under the correct tap and fill his order.

Grabbing a napkin when I'm finished, I hand the cup to him. "Anything else I can get you?"

Leaning in so only I can hear what he confidently suggests, "I'd love a dance later if you're able to get away."

As nice as the gesture is, I'm not interested. First, I don't become a sudden guest at events I'm working and two, Derek.

"I don't think that's such a great idea," I say, trying to politely get out of it.

"Why's that? You're allowed to take a break, aren't you? I mean... my sister's the bride. I can talk to her if you think it'll be an issue. She mentioned you were single."

Yeah, still not happening. "The issue is that not only am I working, but I'm exclusively seeing someone."

He juts his chin out indignantly. "Is that so?"

"Neither Derek nor I are into sharing, so it works out for us," I say, leaving no room for argument.

The moment the words fall from my lips, I spot Nita standing next to me, and she gives me a knowing look that clearly says she wants to repeat the groomsman's question.

Holy shit, did I just say that?

Defeat is clear in his expression as his shoulders round slightly. "Okay, then. Thanks for the drink."

"Enjoy your evening," I say as I would to any other guest before turning my attention to Nita.

Her cocky expression says it all. "So you're not into sharing, are you? Since when did you date anyone exclusively?"

"Since I made an agreement with Derek," I deadpan, trying to not give her any ammunition.

"But you said he is leaving soon."

"When he leaves in October, I'll go back to casual hookups that only happen once in a blue moon and my usual no-strings lifestyle."

Nita's brows lower as she draws out my name as if she's admonishing me. "Tessa…"

"What?" I say defensively. "I only speak the truth. You know I don't do long-term relationships. Hell, I barely have time to have a relationship with my trusty vibrator. Besides, Derek is leaving, so this is the perfect arrangement. I get great sex on the regular, and it has an expiration date in place. I know the stakes; it's not like I'm suddenly going to catch feelings for him or anything."

Shaking her head, she sighs, "Oh, Tessa."

Not needing her pity, I switch gears. "If you had the opportunity to have a no-strings-attached fling with Jake, would you? I mean, you know he's going back to school, so there's an expiration date. I wouldn't blame you a bit for wanting to experience the best sex of your life—over and over —while it lasts. Then when he goes back to school, you can go on with your life, knowing that you'd taken a chance and lived for once."

"The best sex of my life, you say? I've only kissed him— today. I have no idea if the sex will be good." Then she pats me on the shoulder. "Good luck on that not-catching-feelings part. I'm not sure I could walk away from the best sex of my life— nor would I want to."

Fuck. Had I just admitted that sex with Derek is the best of my life?

# Chapter 11

## Derek

NOT WANTING to cancel my appointment with Dax, I've taken the earliest flight available to guarantee I'll back to Bear Creek on time. I've been up since three, Portland time, and as I sit here, listening to the tattoo gun buzz, I find my eyes blinking longer than necessary. The only thing that's keeping me awake in this moment is the fact that Tessa is due any moment, and I'll never hear the end of it if she pops in and I'm sound asleep.

Thanks to a flight delay, I had to drive straight from the airport. I haven't seen Tessa in over a week and as the time gets closer to her arrival, I'll admit after not seeing her for so long, I'm anxious.

I've had plenty of time to think about things both on my flight home and as I've sat my ass in this chair. I'm not sure why, but watching my brother and sister get married within weeks of each other has made me take stock of things and truly evaluate what I want for myself. I've always thought I'd been completely content with how things were in my life. Sure, I've had serious as well as casual relationships, but none of them have amounted to needing to spend the rest of my life with someone.

Could I see myself going there with Tessa?

Fuck, just the thought of it makes my chest tighten.

Rubbing at the tightness with my free hand, I squash the thoughts away.

She wants casual.

She *wants* an expiration date.

Even if I do have real feelings for her, my lease is up in a matter of weeks. So, it's a moot point. I'm leaving—and that will be the end of it.

When the bell above the door dings to signal a new customer, my breath catches in my throat. Tessa's wearing a pair of black shorts which accentuates her muscular legs and a blue shirt that makes her gorgeous eyes pop. But that's not what has my tongue sticking to the roof of my mouth. No, that'd be the way she smiles at me, making me feel it all over my body.

God, I want her.

I've been in this chair almost three hours, and we're due for a lunch break soon, hopefully. Knowing my session will last for hours, Tessa has insisted on bringing lunch for everyone. The only thing keeping me in this chair is Dax and his tattoo gun.

I've sat far too long to have him make a mistake now. Glancing at my shoulder, I'm not able to see everything from this angle, but what I can see so far, he more than meets my expectations. Unfortunately, it's also torture knowing Tessa's within my reach and not being able to do anything about it. It was hard enough when she was just a figment of my imagination while on my trip. With each minute that passes, I'd be lying if I said I didn't wish for Dax to be done.

Don't get me wrong, I'm grateful to Tessa for introducing

me to Dax. We met a few times last week, and he was surprised and honored to learn I've had my basic tattoo drawn for almost a year, but haven't found an artist who could pull it off. But after seeing Tessa's ink, I knew without a doubt Dax could do what I had in mind.

To make matters worse, the fragrant foods from the restaurant make me realize I haven't eaten in hours. Watching Tessa from afar, my empty stomach grumbles. Being hungry must cause heartburn, because that spot right under my ribs throbs with each second I wait. Rubbing the pain away, I grin and nod back to Tessa in greeting. She's such a sight for sore eyes.

"Hope you don't mind, I brought more than enough food to feed an army. I wasn't sure who's on shift today."

Dax nods a thanks but stays focused on the ridge of the mountain he's shading.

Seeing Dax busy at work on my quarter sleeve, Tessa makes a beeline for Luna. Luna's another tattoo artist, who's currently sitting at the front desk between customers.

My first impression of Luna was her uncanny resemblance of Kat von D. In my short time I've been here, it's clear she takes no shit from anyone. She's funny as hell and has helped me pass the time by paying attention to her antics while Dax works his magic on my tat.

After putting the food on the counter, Tessa enthusiastically turns and hugs Luna. "It's been so long. What's new with you?"

Luna replies something I don't quite catch, and the two of them roll their eyes and continue chatting about something else. With Dax concentrating on this intricate part of my ink, I find myself being entertained at the sight of Luna and Tessa as they animatedly talk with their hands.

Who am I kidding? My focus is on Tessa. It's great to see her in her element with her friends. One thing I've quickly learned about Tessa is there isn't a pretentious bone in her body. What you see is what you get, and I love it.

Over the years, I've dated plenty of women who could double as chameleons. A few times, I didn't find out until it was too late, and I was caught by surprise when they showed their true colors. Maybe it's because I'm almost thirty, or with the wrong person, dating can be a daunting task, but I'm so over fake people. Just watching Tessa, I'm reminded of how genuine she is.

When the buzzing suddenly stops, Dax asks, "You ready for a lunch break?"

It takes every ounce of constraint to not bolt to Tessa, while I wait for Dax to cover my arm with Saran wrap. By the time he finishes, my need to touch her is almost uncontrollable.

Before I can act, Dax turns to Tessa. "That food smells fucking fantastic. I almost said fuck it and stopped the moment you walked in—but Derek deserves better, and I wanted to get the ridge right while I was in the zone."

"Yeah, it'd suck to have to cover up fresh ink," Tessa says, pointing to my shoulder as her eyes find mine, and she hops off the stool. "Hey, handsome," has never sounded sexier.

I can't close the distance between us fast enough.

"Hey yourself, beautiful," I tease in return as I snake an arm around her. As soon as we're close enough, I whisper, "I've missed you."

She must feel the same because her lips crash onto mine, and her fingertips trace along the spine of my back. I hadn't bothered putting on a shirt since my priority was getting to her. Cupping the nape of her neck, I deepen our kiss, showing her how much I've missed her.

Fuck. She feels incredible.

Unfortunately, all good things must come to an end. When I hear a stool scrape, I'm reminded that we're not alone. Pulling back, her dazzled expression freezes me in place. Yeah, I wasn't the only one affected by this kiss.

She lifts up onto her toes and whispers so only I can hear, "I'm not done with you yet. Let's go eat so Dax can finish, and I'm one step closer to having my way with you."

Fuck me.

She's like a fantasy and a wet dream all rolled up into one perfect package.

In an effort to keep her close, I link my hand in hers and guide her to our food. Dax or Luna has dragged up an additional stool, which means one of us will have to stand. Since my ass has been in a seat all day, I offer it to Tessa.

Tessa has brought a variety of sandwiches for us to choose from, as well as bags of chips and bottles of root beer. I grab a chicken salad sandwich and settle next to her at the counter.

"How was your flight?" she asks just as I take a large bite of my sandwich.

"It wasn't too bad. I did take pity on this poor mom who juggled three kids under the age of five," I admit when my mouth is empty.

"How so?" Dax asks.

"Well, I saw them struggling in the airport. She had a baby strapped to her, a toddler, and a boy who proudly told me he was five. She'd purchased a seat for the infant, so she could use her car seat, but that meant one of them had to sit next to me across the aisle."

Dax cringes, and I chuckle at his absurdity. "Nah, man. It wasn't bad at all. Growing up as the oldest of four, I remember trips with my siblings—as well as the horror stories Mom used to tell about taking us places on her own when Dad couldn't go the entire time. So, I offered to help."

Tessa raises an eyebrow but says nothing.

"Just as the plane got up in the air, her baby fussed, and her youngest had to go to the bathroom. Knowing how tight of a space it is in those bathrooms alone, I offered to hold the baby while she helped her toddler."

"Seriously?" The words fly out of Luna's mouth. "She just handed you a baby?"

"Well, her family and I had been talking all through the boarding process, and it's not like I was going anywhere..." I shrug. "I'll admit I don't have a lot of experience with kids, but I'm not incompetent. With the help of her older brother Alden, I got little Kennedy settled in no time. He showed me what his dad does to soothe her and before I knew it, she was fast asleep in my arms."

"No shit..." Dax says in awe.

"Yeah, it was crazy. But when her mom came back, I almost woke her up by laughing at the strange expression on her face. She'd told me Kennedy had been fussing for hours, and I must have the magic touch. She tried to transfer

Kennedy into her arms, but she started to fuss. The moment I patted her little back, she went right back to sleep. Seeing the sheer exhaustion on her mom's face, I offered to hold her until she woke up. You would've thought I'd just given her a million bucks."

"How long did she sleep?" Tessa asks with interest.

"Uh... shit... I don't know. I think we had about twenty minutes before we landed. So, a couple of hours? Fuck, I don't know. Once Alden fell asleep in the seat next to me, I just read on my phone to pass the time."

Luna leans in, pounding the table between us. "You seriously held a stranger's kid for hours while it slept?" Then she looks to Tessa. "You said he had brothers, right? Any chance I could meet one?"

"Uh, Damien is off the market as I was just in his wedding this weekend. Davis is available, but he's pretty much married to his career as a med student."

"Damn. What about cousins?" Luna asks with interest.

"I've got a lot of girl cousins, but most of the guys are either married or still not legal yet."

Luna rolls her eyes, feigning disappointment. "Tessa said you were the best man in the wedding?"

"Yeah, apparently, wedding fever is catching in my family." I roll my eyes at the thought.

"What's that mean?" Luna asks.

"Well..." I start but am unsure of where to begin. "My sister just pulled off a surprise wedding at the beginning of July and in the last month, my brother's not only gotten engaged to a woman none of us knew he was seriously dating… but now they're married, too."

Dax lets out a low whistle. "That's definitely the fast track."

I nod in agreement. "But just seeing the two of them together, you know it's gonna last. I couldn't be happier for him."

"Tell them what you told me about their officiant Jack," Tessa demands. "I almost died."

"Ohmigod. That man was a riot. I'm so glad I met him." So many one-liners that flew off that man's lips this weekend, it's hard to know where to start. But taking a deep breath, I back up and start at the beginning.

"My brother met his wife Vanessa at the diner she worked at. According to the stories I was told this weekend, he returned each morning for more than the food. Though in Jack's words, the poor girl was clueless. She'd been so focused on raising Jules—her five-year-old—that she didn't think any man would be interested. According to Jack—she was dead wrong. Lucky for Dame, she noticed him. Jack was a regular patron, and he went on and on at the rehearsal dinner about how he'd worry his coffee would get cold by the time she got around to refilling his cup.

"You see, Jack is this prickly old man who calls it just as he sees it. But everyone knows under that grumpy exterior, he's got a heart of gold. When Vanessa's brother, Vince, walked her down the aisle, Jack made it very clear to Dame that Vince may be giving her away, but if he was to pull any funny business, Jack himself would take care of things. He not so subtly reminded Dame that he grew up in the South and knew how to hide a body. I'm telling you, the entire yard erupted in laughter when my brother just gulped, too stunned for words. I swear you could hear a pin drop until Jules said, loud enough for everyone to hear, 'Really? Will you teach me that trick? I always get caught at hide and seek.' I don't think anyone has ever laughed harder than I did in that moment. Like seriously—tears rolled down my face."

"Holy shit." Luna gasps. "That's hilarious."

"Oh, you haven't heard the best part yet," Tessa assures the room.

"Nope," I agree. "That would be at the end of the ceremony. Dame and Vanessa had just said their vows, and we're all waiting for them to kiss and seal the deal. Before he tells Damien to kiss the bride, I shit you not, he leans in, places a hand on my brother's shoulders, and says, 'Now, remember, son, this is a PG show, so keep what I'm about to tell you family friendly.' Then he cleared his throat and said, 'You may kiss your bride.' Everyone cracked up before Dame and Vanessa kissed—which of course, he made a show out of causing everyone to only laugh harder."

"God, I wish I could've seen that." Tessa holds a hand over her stomach as she silently shakes, fighting back laughter.

"I don't plan on getting married anytime soon, but I want a man to kiss the fuck out of me when I do," Luna says before taking another bite of her food.

"No kidding," Tessa agrees, leaving me to wonder exactly which part she agrees with, waiting for marriage or getting properly kissed.

I don't get time to ponder it because the subject is quickly changed back to my tattoo and how much longer Dax thinks it will take to get it completed. Soon, Dax excuses himself to do something in the back room, and I use this moment to use the restroom and stretch my legs. By the time I return, Tessa's packing up the remaining things and getting ready to leave.

When the phone rings, and Luna's attention is elsewhere, I snake an arm around Tessa from behind. Leaning in, I kiss her neck. "Mmmm... you taste amazing..."

"Don't start something you can't finish," she whispers so only I can hear as her ass presses into me.

"Trust me, beautiful. I'm gonna finish... but we'll have to wait until we're alone."

When Dax walks back into the room, he asks, "You ready to get back at it?"

Looking to Tessa, I smile. "Yep." Then I whisper to her, "Why did we make plans for dinner tonight?"

Rolling her eyes, she turns to face me. "Because Nita and I have a standing dinner date. Be thankful we've decided to bless you with our presence."

I'll gladly take any time I can get with Tessa. Leaning in, I kiss her once more. "I'll text you when I'm on my way home."

# Chapter 12

## Tessa

"WHAT TIME DID you say he was getting here?" Nita says as she takes another sip of her margarita.

Since the tattoo is taking longer than expected, Derek encourages me to meet Nita for drinks like expected, and he'll catch up with us as soon as he can.

"I'm not sure, but if he doesn't show up soon, we'll order without him. I'm starving." He'll understand. Though it's been over four hours since I brought him lunch. Maybe I should text him and order something for him.

**Me: Want us to order something for you or should we wait until you get here?**

His reply is instant.

**Derek: I'm leaving my apartment now. I had to stop at home for a clean shirt. Apparently… Kennedy left a drool stain this morning, and I hadn't noticed until Luna pointed it out.**

Oh, my heart. Is it possible for ovaries to burst?
Don't get me wrong, I'm nowhere ready for kids, and I'm

terrified of having them, but that doesn't mean I can't appreciate the fact he willingly let a stranger's five-month-old baby sleep on his chest for the better part of his flight.

"What's got you smiling like a lunatic over there?" Nita asks, interrupting my thoughts.

"It's nothing, Derek will be here in a few minutes."

"Uh-huh..." she draws out. Clearly, she thinks I'm full of shit, but how exactly do I explain I'm smiling about baby drool? She'll have me committed, for sure.

Quickly, I type out a message then stow my phone.

**Me: We'll wait for you. Drive safe.**

When I look up, Nita's still staring at me.

"What?" I pat down my face to see if I'd dripped salt or something.

"If that's how we're playing it, I'll let it go—for now."

Okay. Maybe she's the one losing it as I have no idea what she thinks I'm hiding from her. Instead of dwelling on me, I turn the tables. "So, have you seen any more of Jake?"

Suddenly, her drink is extremely interesting, and my always put-together friend blushes. Her lips purse, and her cheeks turn as red as a tomato. What the fuck is up with that?

Unable to help myself, I pry, "What aren't you telling me?"

"Oh... I've definitely seen him."

"Like you've run into him at the grocery store? Or..." I pause for effect. "In the biblical sense?"

Her cheeks manage to turn a darker shade of red as her

teeth bite into her lower lip so hard, I swear she'll need stitches if she keeps it up.

Clearly, the girl's been holding out on me, and my imagination's running wild. But knowing my best friend, I just sit as patiently as I can and wait her out. She always caves under the pressure of silence. It's almost comical to watch her implode and eventually word vomit her entire life's story if she thinks you don't believe her.

Casually, sipping on my margarita, I pretend to check the clock on my phone as the seconds tick by.

It's almost commendable that she lasts nearly a minute before the words tumble out of her mouth.

Gulping in a large breath of air, the dam breaks. "I didn't intend to... but we... slept together last night."

Okay. I'd been joking about knowing him in the biblical sense. I thought at most, she'd at least agreed to go on a date or perhaps kiss. But sleep with him? This is so unlike her.

Nita slaps me on the shoulder. "Oh, get your jaw off the floor; it's not like I'm a virgin."

"But Saturday, you said he'd only hit on you..." I draw out. "Was there something else you hadn't told me?"

"No, we'd only kissed before I left to help you at the wedding. But when I got back, the guys were still hanging at the house. We all started talking. Eventually, everyone started to leave. Shane left to take a girl he'd been seeing home and with the look on his face, I knew he had no intentions of returning. The next thing I knew, it was just Jake and me."

"But that was Saturday night. You said you slept with him last night. I'm confused."

I want to die laughing when Nita whisper-shouts at me, "Let me paint a clearer picture. We slept together technically Sunday morning, spent the freaking day together out of the house so Shane wouldn't see us, and he slept over last night again."

"I take it you're over your adversity to dating younger men?" I tease.

Her smile is almost dreamy as she sighs. "God, Tess... I'm so over it. I'd be missing out on so much if I'd ignored my feelings for him." Then her expression darkens. "But we still haven't figured out how to tell Shane."

"From that look on your face, Jake will be coming around often. It's probably best to not sneak around. The truth always comes out. Besides, he's bound to notice if his buddy's rig is in the driveway, and he's nowhere to be found." I laugh at the thought. Maybe this margarita is getting to me.

"Speaking of good sex..." Nita tips her head in the direction behind me. "Your ride for the night just got here."

My eyes nearly bug out as I nearly spit out my drink. "What the fuck? Have you been day drinking?" Clearly, she has, and her inhibitions are going, going, gone if she's openly being suggestive. She's not a prude—or we couldn't be friends. But she's usually not so bold either. *Maybe a good weekend of sex will do that to you.*

Innocently, Nita shrugs. "What? I thought he was taking you home tonight. Jake's decided to be my DD tonight. I guess we can drive you home, too, if you need a ride."

Oh, that girl knows exactly what she's doing.

She smirks, then smiles a warm greeting to Derek. "Hey, Derek. How's the arm feeling?"

He looks at his wrapped arm peeking out from his loose t-shirt. "It feels like one hell of a sunburn, but it looks freaking amazing. I just have to keep it wrapped for a few more hours, then the world can see it."

"Do you want to eat here at the bar or move to a table?" A waitress interrupts now that our party is here.

After looking to Derek and me, Nita answers for all of us, "Here in the bar is fine."

This isn't the first time Derek and Nita have met, but it's the first time it's only been the three of us. It's like we're all old friends as we fill him in on the wedding we went to, while he tells Nita about his brothers. Before I know it, I've had my third margarita, and we've finished our meal.

As we get close to finishing the last of our drinks, I notice Nita pull out her phone and text someone. She doesn't even have to say a word, to know that Jake will be here soon—it's written all over her face.

Since Nita lives close, we'd walked to the restaurant. When we all stand to leave, Derek asks, "Am I dropping you home?"

In that moment, Jake walks into the bar, and we may as well be invisible. He walks straight up to her and plants a long kiss on her. So much for keeping things on the down low. I sure hope they tell Shane soon. Bear Creek may be growing in population, but it's still small enough for rumors to fly.

We go through introductions between Jake and Derek, but I can tell from the exhausted expression on Derek's face that he's spent from traveling and spending the day getting his tattoo. Besides, I want some time alone with my man. He's been gone nearly a week, and snuggling with him sounds just about perfect.

As soon as it's socially appropriate, we make our excuse to leave. From the appreciative look on Nita's face, I'm positive I'm not the only one looking forward to time with my man tonight.

*My man? When did Derek become my man?*

I don't get a chance to contemplate that realization. As soon as we're outside the restaurant, Derek pulls me to the passenger side of his Range Rover. He opens my door, but before I can step inside, he pulls me close and kisses me as if he's a blind man seeing color for the first time.

He must've put on fresh cologne when he stopped by his apartment; his delicious scent has been assaulting me all night —in the best possible way. The way his tongue slides across my lips as his hand slides up my spine, has me needing to climb him like a tree But when a car door shuts nearby, I'm reminded we're still in public.

Breaking the kiss, I smile against his lips. "I take it you're not ready for bed when we get home."

"Oh, Tess, I'm ready for bed, but I have no intentions of sleeping," he practically growls.

"Now that's something I can get on board with, handsome."

I've never been more thankful that we live only mere minutes away.

# Chapter 13
## Derek

EVERY MINUTE I spend with Tessa is never enough. Somehow, over the past few weeks, we've managed to adult during daylight hours, but at night, we're wild and carefree as we fulfill every possible fantasy we can come up with. I love how creative her mind is and how responsive her body becomes.

Fuck me, I don't think I'll ever get my fill of her.

She's downstairs in her apartment getting ready, while I finish up a few things, so I can relax and enjoy our weekend. The plan is for us to watch the pre-season game between Denver and the Rainier Renegades with Dani, my brothers, and Vanessa in the suite reserved for the team. Dani concocted this plan as soon as I moved to Bear Creek. Though no one expected Dame to tie the knot mere weeks ago.

My brothers and I are looking forward to some brotherly bonding as we hike along the trails Tessa has shown me. Luke's bummed out he can't join us; he has to travel back with the team in the morning. With the team staying the night, Luke has insisted on planning a family dinner this evening after the game, so he won't miss out on everything.

Dani and Vanessa insist on a girls' day while we do our brotherly bonding. I'm looking forward to showing my family

Colorado. I'm grateful for them extending their stay to make it a long weekend.

Knowing we need to get this show on the road, I gather the last of the things I think we'll need and lock up. Wanting to give Tessa the time she needs, I drop things off in the Rover before knocking on her door.

When the door swings open a few seconds later, my jaw drops to the floor in shock. She's wearing a pair of jean shorts which accentuate her sexy-as-fuck legs and a devilish smirk. But that's not all. Nope, the vixen is wearing a Denver shirt.

"Uh... you do know we'll be going to dinner tonight with the head coach of the Rainier Renegades, right?"

The smart ass just nods, raising her chin indignantly.

"We'll also be sitting in a suite with families of the team— you will be the *only* person wearing the wrong colors."

"Who says they're the wrong colors?" she challenges, and I want to kiss that smug smirk right off her face. "You're in my country. Not the other way around."

She has a point.

Instead of arguing, I just stare, hoping she'll change her mind.

When she asks, "Are you ready to go?" I realize I'm being ridiculous. If she's okay and prepared to be ridiculed, it's not my problem. After all, it's just football, and a little friendly competition never hurt anyone.

You'd think I'm the long-lost brother who hasn't been seen in years from the way my sister greets us outside the stadium. Maybe it's her pregnancy hormones, but Dani's a little over the top, even for her. She tears up when she pulls me in for a hug.

Once she releases me from her vise grip of a hug, I quickly introduce Tessa. My sister has apparently become a master hugger, because she hugs Tessa just as fiercely, knocking her off guard. When they pull apart, I quickly make introductions to the rest of my family.

Tessa congratulates Damien and Vanessa as well as Dani on their recent marriages. Then she turns to Davis and asks, "How's your latest residency?"

As Davis answers, both Damien and Dani look to me with wide eyes.

Telepathically, I answer their unspoken question with a quick nod.

*Yes, she's important enough to know our family.*

Dani throws a palm over her chest, and I swear tears prick her eyes, making me wonder *who the hell is this woman and what have they done with my sassy sister?*

When the usher opens the suite for the owner and families who've made the out-of-town trip, all eyes land on Tessa. Mike Townsend, the freaking owner of the Rainier Renegades, steps in with a stern look on his face.

"And just who do we have here?"

Tessa doesn't miss a beat. She steps forward to shake his hand and says, "It's a pleasure to meet you, Mr. Townsend. I'm Tessa Sinclair. I hope you're enjoying Denver. If you ever get the chance to drop into Bear Creek, I'd be happy to extend my gratitude for these amazing seats. Stop by my microbrewery Bed Knobs & Brews, and you'll be treated well. Since you're in *my neck of the woods,*" she says with emphasis, "I'll be happy to show you around."

"Holy shit, she has balls," someone I don't know says in the suite.

To my surprise, Mike Townsend belly laughs. Full on, rattle the walls type of laugh, making the entire suite join him. "Well, Tessa, I might take you up on that next time I'm in town. I've gotta say... with cojones like that, you're welcome here anytime." Then he turns his attention to Dani. "It's great to see you, Dani. I'm glad your family could make it."

When Mike gets to me, he leans in so only I can hear, "That one's a keeper, son. Don't let her get away."

As we find our seat, his words eat at me.

From the corner of my eye, I see Damien pull Vanessa in and kiss the top of her head. Sure, Tessa and I have an easy relationship like that, but what I don't understand is how he just knew Van was the one for him.

Here I am, the oldest, and I'm the only one who doesn't have a clear path set out for myself.

What the fuck is wrong with me? Did I miss the commitment gene or something?

Dani has her books, Luke, and a baby on the way. Damien's a civil engineer for the largest job on Columbia River University's campus. He knew almost instantly that Vanessa was the one for him. But what I don't get is, *how* did he know? She came with a built-in family, so now my younger brother's also a dad. Don't get me wrong, he'll be a great one, but *how did he know?*

The only calling I've focused on is starting my own business. At twenty-nine, I've just taken the biggest risk of my life and set out on my own as a freelance designer. It could be a total bust, and I'll be back at square one all over again.

When Tessa reaches over and squeezes my thigh, I'm brought out of my funk. "You okay?"

"Yeah, sure." I quickly dismiss, but deep down, I know I want what my brother has. The problem is, I have no fucking clue how to get it.

# Chapter 14
## Derek

THANKFULLY, I don't have time to dwell on those thoughts once the game starts. Denver quickly takes the lead, causing Tessa to cheer proudly, and the rest of the room gives her the stink eye, but we could care less. In the next play, the Renegades score. The score goes back and forth, and by halftime, it's tied.

As Luke runs off the field with his team, Dani looks to the rest of us and pretends to wipe the sweat from her brow. "I don't know about you, but that was freaking intense."

"It sure was," Vanessa agrees, then she whispers conspiratorially, "How have you not started writing sports romance with all this as inspiration?"

Dani looks around to make sure no one but us can hear. "Would you believe I never watched sports until I met Luke?"

When Vanessa's eyes widen and looks around at all three of us brothers, Damien breaks the silence. "I know you may be a super fan of my dear sister in her author world, but trust me, this woman knows very little about sports."

Dani rolls her eyes and shrugs. "It's true. I even got jealous of Sean Peters for getting handsy with Luke—and his only job is to be a line coach, ensuring Luke stays off the field so the team doesn't get fined."

"That's hysterical." Tessa laughs. "I'll have to pay closer attention to Luke when the game resumes to see who this guy is. I've been so focused on the players, I hadn't noticed. But for the record, I love your books, and I think you could pull off at least football as a sports romance—with the help of Luke as a reference. You're super talented, and I'm sure you could write anything you set your mind to."

"But won't my readers..." Dani starts, but Van and Tessa cut her off.

"Girl, they will follow you anywhere," Tessa says.

While Van spits out, "They love you."

"Maybe..." Dani says as then she zones out like she does when those plots run loose in her mind.

As guys and her brothers, we're used to it, but obviously the girls look to us with concern when she doesn't answer. Davis interrupts, "Don't mind Dani, that's just the hazards of being around her—she gets stuck in her head. Don't worry, she'll come out of it soon—unless she digs out her notebook. Then we'll probably talk to her again when the game is over."

"I'm not that bad—and I'm right here," Dani protests.

Damien looks to his wife and mouths, "Yes, she is." And the rest of us who were paying attention burst out into laughter.

When the team returns to the field, and the game resumes, our conversations slow down. After a while, I almost spit out my drink when Vanessa giggles. "I finally get what Sean meant at your wedding when he said he got handsy with Luke. They don't show that on TV."

"That's because they focus on the game, not the coaches,"

Damien whisper shouts. "Did you even see that last play? Our new quarterback is gonna have an amazing season if he keeps playing like that."

"No kidding," I agree. "I can't wait to see where this season takes us."

The game is a freaking nail biter for the rest of the second half. All of us are on our feet with each play. When there's less than twenty seconds left in the game, the Renegades make a field goal, bringing us out of a tie.

I swear when Denver takes repossession of the ball, those ten seconds on the clock last a lifetime. They make some momentum by catching two back-to-back passes, causing first downs. Of course, this stops the clock, and we have to wait on bated breath to see if the Renegades defense can hold them off on the next play.

On the third down, there's only three seconds left on the clock. The ball is snapped, and our defensive end plows through their line, leaving the quarterback exposed. Two steps later, and Denver's quarterback is sacked as the buzzer echoes through the stadium. The entire room erupts in cheers as the sounds from the stadium reverberate through the walls. For a game on the road, the Renegades sure have a lot of fans in attendance.

"And that's how the game is played!" I holler in excitement as I turn to Davis, giving him a fist bump, then pat Tessa on the back. "Your O-line needs some work if Sanders doesn't want to spend the season on his backside."

Rolling her beautiful eyes, her lips quirk. "Our O-line is just fine. Thank you very much."

*Clearly, that wasn't the case in this instance.*

Before I can say anything, Tessa quickly adds, "Besides, it's only the pre-season. We've got time to get the kinks worked out."

"If you say so," I deadpan. "The Rainier Renegades were on fire today. You'd better watch out."

"If you come to another game, we'll have to get you a Renegades jersey," Dani adds. "If I can be converted into a fan, I'm sure we can convert you, too."

Knowing we have to wait for Luke, we continue to talk about our favorite plays of the day, while the crowd disperses. We let Tessa get in her few moments of glory, but in the end, we not so subtly point out—the best team won. It's Luke's team after all.

As we're following Damien to the restaurant that Luke has made reservations, Davis asks from the back seat, "Where the hell did Luke make reservations? We've been driving for nearly forty minutes, and I'm starving."

"At least we won't have far to drive when we return to Bear Creek," I offer as a consolation. We're well over halfway back.

When we finally pull off the highway and exit the car, Davis mutters so only I can hear, "Geesh, I thought I was getting away from the lovey-dovey newlyweds by riding with you. But you and Tessa are just as bad with your constant hand holding. I'm totally a seventh-wheel."

"Oh, Davy, are you feeling left out?" I tease condescendingly. "I can hold your hand, too, baby brother."

"I'll pass," he grumbles. "I thought you'd be my wingman

while you're here. I don't get much time off, and I could use a good night out."

"I'll tell ya what," I offer as a compromise, knowing exactly how he feels. "Tomorrow, after we go hiking, I know a great place to grab some beers. Who knows, maybe you'll meet someone."

Once inside, we don't even have to wait to be seated. Luke's reserved a table in the back of the restaurant that will give us privacy and room to be the boisterous group we can be when we're together.

Soon after we arrive, Dani says she needs to use the restroom, and the next thing I know, the girls are all taking advantage. They give us their order for drinks, and we make small talk until they return.

At first, the conversation is about the game, but eventually, it turns to Damien's job on campus, and Davis's rotation at the hospital in Oregon. By the time the women return, the conversation has turned to me.

"So, Derek," Luke says, after taking a sip of his Coke. "We didn't get the chance to catch up at Damien's wedding. How's the new business venture going?" Luke had only flown in for the wedding itself, then left that evening to be in Arizona for the pre-season opener. He may have lived in Washington for the past ten years, but sometimes he still sounds like he's living in Nashville.

"It's going well. I've almost completed the project I've relocated for, and the rest of my clientele keeps growing. Working for myself may have some risks, but so far, the rewards have outweighed them."

"Where will you go next? You can work from anywhere, can't you?" Davis asks innocently. He has no freaking clue that's the million-dollar question I ask myself daily. The plan is to return to Seattle, but the more time I spend with Tessa, I question my reason for leaving.

Not wanting to see Tessa's reaction, I force myself not to look at her as I reveal, "As long as I have internet and my computers, yes, I can."

"That's the beauty of working for yourself," Dani beams. As an independent author, she can literally work anywhere in the world. "But you've got your house in Seattle. I thought your plans were to return in a few months."

Thank you, captain obvious. The last thing I need is to be reminded Tessa and I have an expiration date. My breath hitches in my throat, and all I can do is shrug in response.

Instead of answering, I ask Vanessa, "Speaking of living anywhere, did you all get Julia settled in her new room?"

Damien's smile is bigger than Vanessa's, but she answers, "Yeah. We moved in to his house right after the wedding. Vince, being the sap that he is, insisted on keeping a room at both houses. In fact, that's where she's staying this weekend." Suddenly, she looks at her watch, then to Damien with wariness. "Speaking of Jules, we need to video chat with her before her bedtime."

She starts to get up, but I quickly interject, "Do you mind if we talk with her? Vince can't monopolize her forever. Eventually, she needs to understand she didn't just get a dad, but inherited three uncles, too."

"And an auntie," Dani throws in for good measure. She'll never let us outshine her.

Glancing around the room, she assures we mean it before putting through the call.

With the call on speaker, we hear it ring twice before an excited Julia fills the room. "Hey, Momma. We watched the game. Luke's team won. Did you see it?"

"Yes, baby. In fact, he's right here. Do you wanna say hi?"

"Yes," she says indignantly. "I *need* to talk to him." The way she says it has us all stifling our laughter.

Vanessa turns the phone to Luke so he can see Jules for himself. "Hi, sweetheart." Luke's Southern drawl shows when he uses the endearment.

Through the phone, I see Jules punch her hips and look as stern as possible, for a five-year-old. "Why did ya have ta make that game so loud? Unks and Syd kept yelling at the TV, and I had to keep asking what was wrong."

Luke's eyes nearly bug out of his head as he clasps a hand over his face to keep from laughing. Of course, that only makes the rest of us in the room laugh louder. Eventually, Luke must think of something to say. "I'll do my best to not make it such a close game in the future."

"Momma says today's game was far away. But if you're my uncle now, does that mean I might get to go to a game someday? I like watching that boy kick the ball into the air real far. I'm sure it's farther than what I see on TV."

Vanessa looks mortified, but Luke reaches out to squeeze her hand beside him. "I'll tell you what, next time there's a home game, if it's okay with your momma, I'll arrange for you to come out on the field before the game starts. Then you can meet some of the players before you watch the game."

"Really? I'll get to do that?" she says in disbelief.

"I'll make it happen, sweetheart," Luke says, then whispers to Damien, "Y'all better be using those season tickets I got for the family. I'll be sure to add some in for Vince and Sydney."

Vanessa mouths, "Thank you," as Damien nods in agreement.

Taking this opportunity, I pull the phone from Luke. "Hi, Jules. Do you remember me?"

Her smile makes my heart melt. "Yep. You're Derek. You like to draw, like me. I got your picture in the mail. Momma put it in a frame, and it's in my new room in Dame's house."

"Our house," Damien corrects as Davis reaches for the phone from me.

"Uncle Davy wants to talk now, Jules. So, I'll say goodbye. I'll check in with you soon."

I hear a "Bye," as she disappears from view.

Davis says, "Hey, Jules. I'll stop by for dinner when I get back. I just wanted to say hi, and I miss you."

"I miss you, too, Davy. Can I talk to Momma now?"

Handing the phone to Vanessa, we all hear, "That sure is *a lot* of uncles. Are you having fun with them?"

"Yes, Sweet Girl, I am. I'd better get going because our dinner is here," Vanessa says as our server places the food we've ordered on the table.

"Good night, Momma. I love you. Before I go, I gotta see Dame."

"I'm right here," Damien says, getting closer to Vanessa. "What's up?"

"I just wanna to say I love you and good night, Daddy."

"Good night, Sweet Girl. We'll call you in the morning. Be good for Vince and Sydney, 'Mkay?"

Oh. My Freaking. Heart. I swear my breath gets clogged in my throat as I watch Damien's eyes fill with tears.

Fuck, who knew those simple words could nearly do me in?

As I look around the table, I can tell we're all thinking the same thing. We just witnessed an incredible moment.

I want this. I want the wife, the two point five kids, and the picket fence. No, fuck the picket fence... and what the hell is a half child anyway? No—I want a future with someone. I want to settle down and know I've found my person. When Tessa's eyes meet mine, I swear if circumstances were different, I could see this future life, with her.

# Chapter 15

## Tessa

THE NEXT DAY, when Vanessa texts to ask if I want to hang with her and Dani for a girls' day, I feel guilty turning them down. Kylie covered a double shift yesterday so I could attend the game, so it's only fair I work her shift today. Thankfully, there's a steady flow of patrons, and I'm forced to be in the work zone, to contend with everything.

Around four that afternoon, I return from doing paperwork in the back room to find Derek and his brothers sitting in a booth. They each have beers in hand and are munching on some appetizers. When Derek's eyes find mine, his smile deepens, sending a shiver down my spine. "Hey, when did you get here?"

"Not long ago." Derek shrugs. "I thought the guys needed to taste the Puckering Pear for themselves when they wouldn't believe how good it was."

Looking to each of his brothers, I see the family resemblance. I know from our time yesterday, they each tower over me. In this light, I also notice they have the same shade of hair, though they each style it differently. Apparently, there's also a Fallon trait of square chins and broad shoulders that's shared as well. As they each smile at me, I'm not surprised to find they each have their own version of a panty-dropping grin, though the only one who has the desired effect is Derek.

"Well, I'm glad you came to the right place. Did Landon set you up with everything you need?"

Since Derek's sitting alone on his side of the booth, he slides over as he asks, "Got time to join us for a bit?"

Knowing everything's covered, I slide in beside him as he leans down, kisses my cheek, and asks, "How's today been?"

I shrug, "It's been busy, but typical for summer."

Damien's expression changes as his eyes zero in on Derek's arm that's stretched out behind me on the booth. He's seen us hold hands and kiss, so why is he scrutinizing this?

"Uh, D?" Damien's voice is filled with uncertainty.

"What's up?" Derek asks as he grabs a tortilla chip and fills it with artichoke dip before plopping it in his mouth.

"When did you get *that*?"

Davis stops mid-chew and looks between Derek and Damien. "I would've noticed at the wedding had I seen it."

Derek chuckles as he pulls up the sleeve of his shirt and proudly shows his new ink the best he can. "I got this the day I got back."

"You got that all in one day?" Davis asks in disbelief.

"One long-ass day," Derek sighs, and I elbow him in the side. "But it was worth it."

"Hmmm…" Damien sighs as he takes a swig of his beer.

"It's sick, D. Makes me think about getting one," Davis says before Damien can finish his thought.

"I know a guy who can hook you up," I offer.

"He does do amazing work," Derek says, replacing his arm behind me on the booth and drapes a hand over my shoulder.

"I'm not sure when I'll be back in Bear Creek." Davis shrugs.

"So what kind of trouble did you boys get into today?" I ask, changing the subject. I'm not sure what Damien's problem is with Derek's ink; he has no problem with mine. In fact, he and Vanessa both mentioned they liked it last night at dinner.

Davis adorably waggles his brows. "Well... if we tell you..."

"You'll have to kill me? Or am I part of the fight club?" I deadpan.

Davis looks to his brothers. They all nod in unison. "Definitely part of the fight club."

"Well, now that I'm part of the club, does that mean I get to go on your next adventure?"

"Unfortunately, I'm flying out at the ass-crack of dawn," Davis mutters. "Don't get me wrong, I want to be a doctor more than anything, but being on vacation has its perks."

"I've convinced Vanessa to have an actual honeymoon. She doesn't know it yet, but I'm whisking her off to New England to see the fall colors."

"Uh... don't ya think as a mom, she might miss her kid?" Derek asks, and I can tell by the look on his face, he doesn't like the surprise factor of Damien's plan.

"I've cleared it with Jules, Vince, and Syd. We're only staying a few more days than planned. Besides, this year, Van's taking on clinicals in her nursing program. She needs all the R&R she can get."

When I spot a line stacking up at the bar, I excuse myself to help out.

By the time I'm able to return, the guys are in deep conversation and don't see me approach. From their tone, it's more serious than when I left.

As I get closer, I hear, "What's going on with you and Tessa, D?" It stops me dead in my tracks.

I know I should let them know I'm here, but for some strange reason, I want to know his answer.

"What do you mean?" Derek says, grabbing a chip from the bowl.

Damien says nothing but waits for his brother to glance up.

While Davis says, "You're looking at her like things are more than casual."

Running a hand through his hair, Derek shrugs. "She and I agreed to an expiration date. We're exclusive while I'm here, and the fact is..." Derek pauses and takes a swig of his beer before continuing. "My lease is up."

"You do remember the point of you becoming your own boss is that you can work from anywhere, right?" Damien says, pointing out the obvious.

Derek's laugh doesn't sound genuine, as he shakes his head. "I know, man. I think Tessa's a great girl, but she and I have an understanding. Besides, I've got a meeting in Seattle with a new client, and I need to check on my house."

I've known this is coming all along, but to hear him say it aloud, makes things final.

When one of their phones signals a notification, I realize I don't want Derek to continue this conversation. So, I make my presence known.

Clearing the sudden lump in my throat, I say more enthusiastic than necessary, "Hey, guys. How's it going? Can I get you anything else while I'm up?"

"Nah, we're good," Damien says as he stands. "The girls just texted, and we're going to meet them in Denver for dinner. Apparently, they've shopped 'til they've dropped, and Dani's too tired to drive out here."

Before I know it, all of the Fallon men are up and standing beside me, so I look to Derek, "Are you going with them?"

"Nah. I'll catch them next time," he says, to my surprise. "They have early flights, so it'll be an early night and a waste of a trip for me."

Davis snakes an arm around me and playfully whispers so everyone can hear, "You keep Derek on his toes... and if you get tired of his sorry ass, remember, I'm the younger and more handsome brother."

"That's only because I'm taken," Damien sighs, elbowing Derek playfully.

"Well... now that you know *both* of my brothers are full of shit, we'll get out of your hair." Derek leans in so that truly only I can hear, "We both know which Fallon you prefer, so there's never been a competition. I'll see you when you get off, beautiful. Let me know if you need anything."

Each of the brothers gives me a hug goodbye, whispering something about their need to get a rise out of Derek. I'll admit, he's adorable when he's trying like hell not to show how annoyed he is.

God, I could get used to this bunch. They always know how to make me laugh.

The moment that thought hits me, another one comes just as fast, and it's like a sucker punch to the gut.

I can't get used to them.

In only a matter of weeks, Derek will be gone, and I'll likely never hear from him again.

# Chapter 16

## Tessa

A LITTLE OVER A WEEK LATER, Derek and I are lying in bed, sprawled across each other with our legs intertwined. It's our last weekend together before he leaves, and we've decided to have a lazy day in bed. Derek's tracing invisible patterns across my back, while my head rests on his chest. In my post-orgasmic bliss, I never want this moment to end.

"You still alive?" Derek asks after I've been quiet for an unusual amount of time.

"Just enjoying the moment."

"I never want this to end." He exhales heavily as I feel him kiss the top of my head.

No kidding. This man reads my body like it's made for him. But with him, it's more, too. The more time I spend with him out of the bedroom, the more my uneasy feeling continues. If he were staying, I'd consider asking for more, but he's not—so I have to deal with reality. In a matter of days, he'll be gone. Therefore, my only goal in this moment is to make the most of my time with him.

If we happen to pass this time naked, you won't hear me complain.

Knowing I can't let myself think about his departure, I quickly pop my head up to look him in the eye and ask,

"Wanna drive up to the Continental Divide? You can't be this close and not see it before you go."

"As long as I get to spend this day with you, I'm game for anything."

"I can order us some food to take for lunch."

I reach for his t-shirt to slip on as I walk to the kitchen to find my phone. Seeing that it's still off, I quickly power it up and think about what else I want to do with Derek while I wait.

Panic strikes when my screen flickers with three voice messages and four text messages from Kylie.

*What the fuck is going on?*

Knowing she'd only call if there is an emergency—especially that many times, I quickly press call instead of taking the time to read or listen to any of her messages.

Kylie picks up on the third ring. "Tessa?"

"Hey, what's up? My phone was off, and I haven't listened to any messages."

Kylie sucks in a huge breath, and it's obvious she's been crying.

"What's wrong, Ky? Talk to me." I force out as I rush to Derek's room to find my pants.

"It's..." She sobs loudly, then takes a fortifying breath and mechanically tells me the details. "It's... my sister. She's stationed in Colorado Springs, but she's been deployed. We just got word that her helicopter has gone missing. It's still unconfirmed, but I need to be with my parents. We might not know for several hours, but there was video of a low-flying Chinook in the area of where it was last located. No one will tell us anything." Her voice breaks, and a sob escapes. "I... I just need my family..." She finally breaks down and sobs once more.

Instantly, I go into survival mode. Ripping my shirt over my head, I search for my bra and find my own shirt from last night. Sensing something is wrong, Derek jumps into action and gets dressed, too.

"What can I do?" I blurt out, making a mental list of all the things I'll need to cover while she's away. "You can't drive in this condition. You're too upset."

"No, I'll be okay. I've got my boyfriend driving me to my parents' place now. They live in Grand Junction. I know Derek's leaving this week, so the timing sucks, but..."

"No buts," I interrupt firmly. "I'll take care of everything at work. You just take care of yourself and your family. Please keep me posted."

"Thank you, Tessa," she starts, then pauses to take a deep breath. "If things go... well, I might need even more time off."

"I've got you covered. Just focus on driving safe and praying for your sister's recovery."

By the time I've hung up the phone, Derek's fully dressed by my side.

"What's going on?" His voice is laced with concern.

"Kylie just called. Her sister's in the Air Force and has gone missing." He had heard the end of my conversation, so I don't bother repeating it.

"That's horrible," Derek says as he pulls me to him. "What can I do?"

Wrapped in his arms, I feel as if I'm protected, and a warm

blanket has been wrapped around me. I wish I could stay in this moment forever.

"There's not much you *can* do. I've gotta pull shifts to pick up the slack while she's gone." My body slags against him, and he holds me tighter.

Taking a deep breath, I'm hit with his delicious fragrance. God, he's standing right next to me, so why do I feel like I miss him already? "This isn't how I wanted to say goodbye to you," I whisper into the universe.

"I know, beautiful. But this isn't goodbye. I still have a few days before I leave. We can see each other when you're not working. You just can't put a restraining order on me if I'm constantly hanging out at Bed Knobs. Since my project is finished, and I've busted my ass to officially carve out this week as a vacation, I do want to spend as much time with you as possible." His hands glide down my spine and cup my ass with a gentle squeeze before he adds, "In or out of bed."

"Trust me." I lean in to kiss him on the lips one last time before having to get to work. "I'd much rather stay in bed with you than face the world this week."

Reality sucks. Not only is Derek leaving in a matter of days, but the thought of what Kylie's family is going through makes my heart hurt even more.

---

YOU KNOW THAT SAYING, when it rains, it pours? That doesn't even begin to describe my last few days. Thanks to a flu virus that took out three of my employees, I was severely short staffed. I've worked from open to close for the past three days, and I'm running on fumes. Derek is a gem. He takes pity on me and busses tables and takes orders when he can. I'm sure this isn't how he wanted to spend his last week here.

The only silver lining in this entire shit show of a week is when Kylie called this morning to say her sister has been found. She's alive but has a broken leg and has been banged up pretty bad. Kylie and her parents have been granted permission to take the next flight to Ramstein Air Force Base in Germany to see her for themselves. I can't blame them. But that also means I'm on my own for another week until she returns. I need to consider hiring more help.

When two hands snake around my torso from behind, I'm startled. That's until I smell Derek's mouthwatering scent, and I completely melt into him. "Relax, beautiful. Your shoulders are gonna hold up your ears if you're not careful."

Sighing, I let my shoulders sag. "I'm trying."

"I wish I didn't have to meet that client on Monday. If I could stick around to help, I would."

"I know," I whisper, but what I want to say is, *that would only put off the inevitable.*

Derek is true to his word this week. We spend every moment I'm not at work together—and it isn't enough. It also doesn't change the facts. He has to leave soon, or he won't get home in time for his potential new client.

When I look into his eyes, his confliction is evident. I know he doesn't want to leave me high and dry, but this new client can put his new company firmly into the black, or so he says. I know firsthand what it's like to take a chance on yourself. There's no way he can pass up this opportunity.

Besides, he has turned in his keys this morning, and there's nothing for him in Bear Creek. His life is in Washington, not Colorado. That's why we agreed to a fling. Whatever has happened between us, has an expiration date—and today is that day.

As I look into his eyes, my stomach clenches, and a wave of nausea hits.

Quickly, I send a prayer to any gods in the universe that might hear my plea this nausea isn't a stomach bug. I can't afford to be sick. I already have Nita coming in to help with the evening shifts, and I've hired some college students, home for the summer to help cover shifts. But they're new—and need training.

"You okay?" Derek asks, brushing a strand of hair from my face.

"Yeah… sure." I have to be.

Neither of us say anything as he takes my hand and walks me out the door to the parking lot. When we're right outside his vehicle, he stops, and we stare at each other for an immeasurable amount of time. Eventually, he's the first to speak.

"Will you call me…" he starts, then looks to the sky before tacking on, "and let me know if you hear more about Kylie's sister," once his focus returns to me.

Leaning in, he kisses me slowly. Knowing this will be our last kiss, I savor the moment and wish like hell it could last forever. He tastes of mint and Derek. Two flavors I honestly don't think I can ever get enough of. Snaking my hands around his neck, I pull him so his body is flush against mine.

When we break apart breathless, I nod. "Yes. I'll call."

An alarm he'd set goes off, and he visibly cringes. "I gotta go. Do you want me to call you?" he whispers.

The words clog in my throat, but I manage a nod.

Fuck, I feel as if I'm about to be sick.

"Okay, then. I'd better hit the road," he says but doesn't let go. Instead, he pulls me tighter, and it takes every fiber of my being not to melt into him.

Knowing I need to say goodbye, I reach up on my toes and press my lips one last time to his mouth. It's a slow and lingering kiss, as if we're memorizing how the other feels. When we break apart, we're both breathless. "You'd better go."

I'm not sure if I'm saying that for his sake or mine. If he doesn't walk away now, he'll never leave, and we'll keep this up.

Wrapping his arms around me in a giant bear hug, he lifts me off the ground. When he sets me down, he whispers, "I can't say goodbye. But I do need to go. So, I'll see you, Tess... someday."

He doesn't wait for me to respond but turns and walks to his Range Rover.

I watch him as he gets in and starts the engine. He doesn't glance my way as he puts the car in gear and drives out of town.

In this moment, I know without a doubt, my life will never be the same without the boy upstairs.

# Chapter 17

## Derek

THE HARDEST THING I've ever had to do in my entire fucking life is drive away from Tessa. I know that if I look at her, I'll probably break down and never leave. To keep her from seeing my watery eyes, I don't draw things out. I could've won an Oscar for the way I pretend she isn't standing outside my door when I drive away. It isn't until I reach the end of the block that I allow myself to look in the rearview mirror, but she is already gone.

I know this thing with Tessa was temporary. She has been adamant that she doesn't have time for long-term or anything serious. I've had casual relationships before and when they end, they end. I walk away unscathed. Simple as that. If my relationship with Tessa is just a temporary thing, why does it feel with each passing mile, my heart is still in Bear Creek?

It doesn't take long before I make it to the highway leading out of town. As I drive into the mountains, my chest tightens, and it gets more difficult to breathe. The altitude must be getting to me. I roll down my window to bring in more air.

It's better, but it doesn't help.

My phone rings, but I can't bring myself to even see who it is, so I let it go straight to voice mail. I just can't people at the moment. If it's important, they'll leave a message.

After a few hours of driving, I spot a small town up ahead. I pull off the highway, knowing this might be my last chance for a while. My shoulders ache as I fill my tank. I must've been vise-gripping the wheel by the stiffness in my fingers. *What the fuck have I been doing?*

I honestly can't tell you a single detail of my trip so far, beyond driving that first block. It's just a string of cars, trees, and long-haul truckers. As I look around, I can see I'm out of the mountains and into the high desert. I've made reservations outside of Boise, and if I'm lucky, I'll be there before midnight.

After my pit stop, my body feels less stiff, but my mind is still a cluster fuck. I can't hold on to a thought for more than a fleeting moment before it drifts away as easily as it comes. Most of which revolve around Tessa. It's probably better that I don't remember everything because recounting every detail of my time with her would be fruitless.

By the time I check into the hotel for the night, I've been driving for over ten hours, and I'm dead on my feet. I take a quick shower and fall into bed. But even my dreams are filled with Tessa, and I wake up searching the bed to hold her.

Christ. I'm so fucked. It hasn't even been a day, and I'm a wreck.

Fuck, it's only three in the morning.

Willing myself to fall asleep so I don't have to add tired to the list of reasons I shouldn't be on the road tomorrow, I toss and turn to get comfortable. Eventually, I must fall asleep; the next thing I know, it's almost eleven in the morning.

*How the fuck did I sleep through my alarm?*

In a panic, I toss back my covers and bolt out of bed. After a quick spin in the shower, I'm dressed and on the road before noon. While filling up my tank, I force myself to look at my messages. Two from Damien, another from my mom. Dani's even left a message, but none are from the only person I want to hear from—Tessa.

I'm sure they'll worry if I don't call them soon, but I'm not in the mood to read a text or listen to my family just yet. I'm sure they'll do everything they can to be supportive, but for now, I'm just not ready to face them. By the time I get home, maybe I'll have more figured out in my head.

About three hours into my trip, my phone rings again. This time it's Davis.

I'm still not ready to talk with anyone, but Davis never calls. I mean, like never. I'm lucky to get a text now and then, but usually I initiate it. Just as I'm about to answer, the ringing stops.

Then it starts again.

Fuck, something must be wrong.

The call picks up through my vehicle's Bluetooth.

"Hey, man, what's up?" I ask, hoping there hasn't been an emergency that I've missed. With all those missed calls from my family, surely, I've missed something.

Fuck. I'm such a selfish prick.

"I don't know. You tell me."

His irritation is laced with concern, which doesn't make any sense.

"What do you mean?" Why would he think something's wrong with me?

"Uh... you've been off the grid for the better part of a day, and I was the designated person from our family group messages to check on you."

"What? Why are y'all group texting about me? You know I've been traveling."

"Uh, because no one has heard a peep from you since you left yesterday. You have Dani's overactive imagination thinking you're dead in a ditch or something, and she's got Mom going now. Pick up your fucking phone, man."

"Oh." That's a far stretch—even for Dani, but I guess I see their point.

"Oh... That's all you've gotta say for yourself. Oh... What's going on, D? This isn't like you."

"I didn't have the best reception."

"Sell it to someone else. You were in Boise last night, not the outer regions of civilization. You're clearly avoiding us—or should I say everyone? Have you spoken to Tessa?"

Just the mention of her name has me rubbing at my aching chest.

"Not since I left," I reluctantly admit.

"Well, at least we knew you were on the road because Dani texted her and asked when you left."

Fuck. "I'm twenty-nine years old. I don't need a babysitter," I spit out in anger.

Though I'm not sure who I'm more upset with, Dani or myself for caring so fucking much.

"Derek, I love you. But if you don't tell me what just crawled up your ass and died, I'm gonna deck you the next time I see you. And you know how protective I am of these hands."

Somehow, my idiotic brother has done something I never thought possible.

He's made me smile. A real one that comes with a genuine laugh.

"I'd like to see you try, brother. But I'm good... or I will be."

Eventually.

"Why do you sound like your favorite set of pens dried up? What's going on? Is it Tessa?"

"What about her?" I ask, sounding defensive even to myself.

"What's going on with her?"

I'm silent for what feels like a full minute before I admit, "Nothing. Nothing's going on with her."

"I don't understand. If nothing is wrong, why aren't you picking up our calls?"

"I don't know..."

"Yeah... and you're so full of shit, your eyes are brown."

"I thought you were the nice one, practicing your bedside manner and all," I remind him.

"Well, everyone's worried sick about you, and I don't have time to beat around the bush... so out with it. I'm fairly certain your sour attitude has everything to do with girl problems. What's going on between you and Tessa?"

Knowing he won't give up, I sigh heavily and give in. "Nothing. That's just it. We agreed to keep things casual when we started this and now that I'm leaving, it's over."

"Do you still feel only *casual* toward her?"

Yeah, Davis doesn't pull any punches.

"No," I sigh heavily, then admit for the first time, "I'm fairly certain I'm in love with her."

Davis chuckles. "Well, that's obvious, but does she know?"

"Nope."

"I thought older brothers were supposed to be the smart ones," he grumbles. "*Why doesn't she know?*" he emphasizes. "The way you two carried on, I thought for certain there might be three weddings in this family this summer."

"What? Why the hell would you think that?" That's absurd.

"Oh, hell, man. You didn't see the way you two looked at each other. It was like she was the earth, moon, and stars all rolled into one. When you breathed in, she exhaled. You were so in sync, I thought you'd already confessed your undying love for one another."

Holy shit. That *is* the way I felt about her. Why the fuck didn't I see that earlier?

"But we agreed it was casual. Her life is in Bear Creek, and mine's in Seattle."

"Wasn't the whole point of you becoming your own boss so you could work from literally anywhere?"

"I know... but... my lease on the apartment was up, and I have a meeting in Seattle with my next client."

"I'm fairly certain I saw other housing options available when I was there... and you can get on a damn plane to meet clients in person. So, cut the crap. I'm fairly certain you've flown to meet clients while living in Seattle, haven't you?"

Fuck. He has me there. "But..."

"But what?" he challenges... "Does she know how you feel?"

She has to, right? I mean, I've shown her. But fuck. We never talked about our arrangement beyond that first week.

"I'll take your silence as a big, fat no."

"We didn't..." Fuck, where do I begin? "She was adamant that she didn't have time for a serious relationship. But I wouldn't take no for an answer. In fact, part of the reason I'm feeling like shit in this moment is because I idiotically promised I wouldn't catch feelings, and this could remain casual because there was a set expiration date."

"You're an idiot, all right. Who agrees to things like that?"

"In my defense, I never thought I'd fall for her. At the time, I wasn't looking for anything serious either, but our chemistry was off the charts, and I couldn't walk away."

"But now you can?" he asks without malice, but all the same, it cuts me like a knife.

"I have to," I sigh heavily in defeat.

"I know you're meeting with a client, but what's the real reason you're coming home?"

Dragging in a hearty breath, I exhale slowly as a million reasons course through my mind, but I stick with the truth.

Reluctantly, I admit, "She didn't ask me to stay..."

# Chapter 18

## Tessa

IT'S BEEN a week since Derek left.

If I didn't have fucking responsibilities, I probably wouldn't even get out of bed. I feel like a Mack truck has hit me at top speed, and I can barely get a breath of fresh air, as I roll through life on autopilot.

Get up, get dressed, work all day, sleep.

Rinse and repeat.

At least this schedule keeps me from thinking.

When I think, it hurts.

To make matters worse, I think I've been fighting off that stomach bug that went through my employees. I have no appetite and when I do eat, my stomach aches even more. Nothing seems to help it either, which just sucks.

Kylie came back yesterday. I'll give her a day or two to get back in the swing of things, then I'm taking some much-needed time off. I'm so relieved her sister is on the mend and is expected to make a full recovery.

To my surprise, Nita comes through the door talking to Kylie and stops dead in her tracks when she sees me.

"Girl, you look like shit," Nita deadpans.

"Well, hello to you, too," I grumble, then get back to work.

"Seriously, what's the matter?" Nita stops right in front of me at the bar.

I look to Kylie and back to my best friend. There's no way I'm saying anything that will make Kylie feel guilty she left. Family is everything, and she has every right to see her sister. "I'm tired," I admit "I didn't sleep well."

"This is more than a bad night's sleep. I've seen you pull all-nighters, then party all day. Don't bullshit me. What's wrong?"

"She's been covering for me," Kylie admits.

But Nita doesn't buy it. "It's more than that. When Tessa opened this place, she worked around the clock. She's got dark circles under her eyes as if she hasn't slept in over a week. If I had to guess, I know the reason, but I'll keep my opinions to myself—for the moment. But I'm more concerned with the fact that she's lost weight since I saw her last."

"Tell me how you feel." *God, with friends like her, who needs enemies.*

"I will... in due time. Why have you been avoiding my calls?"

I totally have. But instead of admitting that, I sternly remind her, "I've been busy."

Squinting her eyes, she crosses her arms over her chest.

After a minute or so of uncomfortable silence, I finally break our apparent staring contest. "What?" comes out more defensive than I intend.

"So, you're saying since Derek left, who used to be connected to you at the hip, and you still had time for me, you haven't had any free time to call or text me back?"

I wince at the mention of his name and rub my aching stomach.

Suddenly, Nita's expression softens. "Oh. Tessa."

Why do I feel as if she's pitying me all of a sudden? I haven't done anything wrong.

When I don't say anything, Nita continues, "You finally caught feelings, didn't you?"

Instinctively, out of self-protection, I deny, "What are you talking about?"

Nita quirks a perfectly sculpted brow at me as if to say, *stop with the bullshit.*

"Derek."

Fuck, I wince again.

Usually, I have a fantastic poker face. But this is Nita, and she knows me.

"And that's what I thought."

Crossing my arms over my chest in self-preservation, I remind her, "He was only here temporarily, and I didn't catch feelings for him."

"If you say so." Disbelief lays clear in her expression.

"I don't do long-term relationships. You know that."

"It's convenient he left then," she snarks.

"Yep." I bite into my lower lip to keep from saying more as the backs of my eyes prick.

"Derek," she whispers.

I flinch as I blink faster, and my nose tingles.

Fuck. She's gonna make me cry.

"Say his name," she urges.

Shaking my head, I bite into my lip harder, and my vision

blurs.

She must walk around the bar to stand next to me; the next thing I know, her arms wrap around me tight as she pulls me into a hug. "It's okay to admit you love him, T. There's nothing wrong with that."

And the dam I've been fighting like hell to hold on to since the moment he left, finally breaks.

Tears roll down my cheeks, and I ugly cry.

Through broken sobs, I finally admit, "I... I love him..." I sniffle. "I... love him... so much.... It hurts." Another sob.

"Ah, honey, that's the only way you can. You're such a strong and fierce woman, but loving someone doesn't make you weak. You know that, right?"

"But... but he left..." God, nothing's been the same since he left.

She's quiet for a long moment as she holds me close and doesn't say anything.

Eventually, she pulls back to look me in the eye. "Did you give him a reason to stay?"

Thinking back through my time with Derek, I realize I never did anything but keep him at arm's length. This only makes me sob harder. "No."

"I know that man loves you, T. I saw it in the way he looked at you each and every time we were together. He made a big point to say one of the biggest advantages of being his own boss is that he can work from anywhere."

"But... he has a home, and his family is in Washington."

A smile plays at my best friend's lips as she shrugs. "There are these amazing inventions called planes. Didn't his family just come for the weekend to see him? I swear, you could prob-ably do the same thing if he lived here, too."

She's so right. Pulling her into a hug, I admit, "God, you're a smart ass, but I love you, Nita."

"Love you, too... you stubborn ass."

When we pull apart, I take a napkin and dry my face.

Straightening my shoulders, I feel much more like myself again. I'm strong and ready to take life by the horns.

Turning to Nita and Kylie, I admit I still need help. "Okay. I've admitted I love him, but now what?"

# Chapter 19

## Tessa

I HAD NEVER EXPECTED when I woke up this morning, I'd be sitting in an Uber by the end of the night. I didn't even go home to pack once the plan was made. I got to the airport with twenty minutes to spare before my flight boarded. Thank God, I didn't have any bags to check because I had to run through the Denver Airport to make it to my gate on time.

Looking at my phone, I've almost texted Derek several times. Somehow, I've managed to stop myself each time, at the last minute. What I need to say needs to be said in person. Simple as that.

He had given me his address a few weeks ago, but I never thought I'd be seeing it in person. At the time, he'd wanted me to ship some of my Puckering Pear when the next fresh batch is made. Shit, I hadn't even thought to bring some as a peace offering.

Now, as I pull onto his street, I wonder if I'm doing the right thing. I don't even know if he's home. But when the Uber stops, I see lights on at his address. His Range Rover must be parked in his garage.

It's dusk, and the sun is setting. From his house, he has an amazing view of Seattle. No wonder he has come home. Compared to this, our apartments are shit.

Just as I'm about to knock, the door rushes open, and I freeze, mid-knock.

God, this man is beautiful. His hair looks like he's been running his hands through it, and his eyes have dark circles under them, but he's still the same beautiful man who left last week.

My chest tightens as I realize just how much I've missed him.

I want to fling myself in his arms, but I'm not sure I'm welcome.

"Tessa?" he asks as if he doesn't believe I'm really here. "What are you doing here?"

My throat is dry as the Sahara Desert, but somehow, I manage to find words. "I came to tell you something."

His brows knit together as he blinks rapidly. "And you couldn't pick up the phone?"

Shit. Maybe I should've called first.

When he takes a step back, I blurt out like the fool I am, "I love you, Derek. I think I've always loved you—well, since that day we went fishing, and you made me dinner, and you made me commit to being in an exclusive relationship with you."

*God, I'm mucking this up.*

I take a deep breath and start again, "But the thing is, I wasn't supposed to love you. You weren't supposed to weasel your way under my skin and make me think I can't live without you. You weren't supposed to walk away and take my heart with you. I've been miserable since you left... and I just now realize it's because I love you. I fucking love you... and now that you're standing there with your mouth hanging open like a fish, I think I'll just shut up now."

Frozen in place, Derek blinks a few times. When I turn to walk away, he reaches out to grab my arm. "Can you repeat that?"

Shit. I've been rambling and have no idea what I'd said. "Uh... which part?"

Grinning, he takes a step closer, and I can feel the warmth of his body wrap around me like a blanket. "The part where you told me you love me."

Smirking, I raise a brow. "I believe I said I fucking love you."

Derek nods. "Good. Because I fucking love you, too."

With that, his lips crash onto mine, and the entire world around me is forgotten.

IT'S funny how life works out. Nearly five years ago, I took a chance on myself and risked it all to start my own business. I moved halfway across the country to help a client, and I wound up finding the love of my life. Not a single day goes by that I don't find myself falling in love with Tessa more.

We still laugh about the night she showed up at my house in Seattle. Not only did she proclaim she fucking loved me for the first time, but it was the start of an amazing adventure for us. Once I got her inside and naked, I fucked her against my front door because the bed was just too far away.

Then we made it to my bedroom, and there in all our naked glory, she asked me to come back to Bear Creek. I said I would—under two conditions. One, that we move out of that shitty apartment and two, she marry me.

I guess Davis was right. There would be three weddings.

Of course, I didn't have a ring or anything. At the time, I wasn't sure I'd see her again. But she's never let me propose again. She still insists to this day that's our engagement story—though we keep the naked parts out—some things are just better kept between us.

Today's another big day for us. As I look around the

crowded room, I see family and friends who've been with us through thick and thin. Even her dad has made the cross-country trek to be here to celebrate with us.

Tessa puts two fingers between her teeth and whistles to gather everyone's attention.

*Yep, that's my girl.*

Then once the room settles, she shouts for everyone to hear, "I just want to say thank you to everyone for coming tonight. From the time Gramps told me about his life being a Bear Creek Runner, I've known I've always wanted to make my own brew. I was thrilled when I opened Bed Knobs & Brew in Bear Creek, and I couldn't be more excited to share my amazingly delicious specialties with all of you in here in Seattle." She looks around the crowd as they cheer before continuing.

"This building may not have once been a bed and breakfast, but it will bear the name just fine. Thank you for being a part of our grand opening."

There are more cheers from our family and friends. "Now, as Gramps always said, let's drink up and may you never see your glass empty."

The crowd goes wild as we all toast the air.

I'm so relieved this day has finally come. It makes me so happy to help make her dreams come true. She's always wanted to open a second location. Since we're always traveling to Washington to visit family for one function or another, it makes sense to do it here. This way, we can be in Colorado for harvest season, so she can make her specialties, and we can still spend time with my family. Her dad even stays with us from time to time now that he's retired.

When Tessa got pregnant with Melody, it made sense for her to take a step back from running the day-to-day things at Bed Knobs. We hired additional help, and Kylie manages the Bear Creek location. Now Tessa just does what she loves best. Overseeing things from afar and making the brew itself. Since we have kept my house in Seattle, we split our time between Seattle and Bear Creek.

Tessa squeezes my hand as she looks into my eyes. "We did it. Can you believe it?"

Needing her lips on mine, I kiss her chastely before responding, "I believe you can do anything you set your mind to. I fucking love you, Tessa."

Grinning from ear to ear, she says, "That's good because I fucking love you, too." Raising her glass to toast this celebration, she says, "Here's to our neighbors fucking like rabbits, so I could meet the boy upstairs."


The End


IF YOU WANT to know how Dani and Damien Fallon found their own happily ever after, be sure to read more in Dani's story—**Making the Call** and **Damien: Book Three in the Perfectly Independent Series**. Don't worry. Davis gets his story, too. **He Saved My Boy** is now available.

https://books2read.com/HSMB

If you'd like a **free** story from me set in this same world - be sure to grab *Snowed In With My Brother's best Friend* to start reading today!

# ABOUT AMANDA SHELLEY

Amanda Shelley writes romantic stories you can escape into. Some are steamy, others are sweet but all have strong characters with a little bit of sass.

When not writing, Amanda enjoys time with her family, playing chauffeur, chef and being an enthusiastic fan for her children. Keeping up with them keeps her alert and grounded in reality. She enjoys long car rides, chai lattes and popping her SUV into four-wheel drive for adventures anywhere.

Amanda loves hearing from readers. Be sure to sign up for her newsletter and follow her on social media. Join her reader's group Amanda's Army of Readers to stay up to date on her latest information.

Readers group: https://www.facebook.com/groups/Amandas ArmyofReaders/
Goodreads: https://www.goodreads.com/author/show/ 19713563.Amanda_Shelley
Newsletter: https://geni.us/AmandaShelleyNL
www.amandashelley.com

# ACKNOWLEDGMENTS

First, I would like to thank you the reader, blogger, and reviewer for taking the time to read this book. There are so many stories to choose from, and I'm humbly honored you've chosen to read mine. I hope you enjoyed Derek and Tessa's story. If you want more from the Fallon family, be sure to check out Dani's and Damien's story. Don't worry, Davis hasn't been left out—his is on the list of stories to write.

I'd love to hear from you and your thoughts about Derek and Tessa. You can find me on social media, my reader's group *Amanda's Army of Readers*, or at www.amandashelley.com. If you care to share your thoughts on this book with other book lovers, please consider leaving a review at any of the retail sites or on Goodreads, BingeBooks, and BookBub.

First, I'd like to thank Sierra Hill for putting together the All American Boys Series. It was so much fun to work with such amazing authors and create this world. What a great way to collaborate personally and professionally. Thank you so much for this experience.

This book wouldn't be what it is without my amazing team of support. To Renita McKinney at A Book A Day Author Services, thank you for helping me develop Derek and Tessa's characters and make them into the best they can be.

To Susan Soares at SJS Editorial Services, thank you for working with me. This book wouldn't be what it is today without you. I appreciate your time and feedback. You're amazing to work with, and I appreciate that you've been with me since the beginning.

To Julie Deaton at Deaton Author Services, thanks for making my book pretty. I appreciate knowing your proofreading is exquisite, and my worries disappear. Your eagle eyes are spectacular, and I don't know what I'd do without you. PS—you can never retire. I'd be so lost without you.

To the people who have supported me along the way, I'm humbly grateful to have you in my life. Whether you've read my books, asked me about my progress, listened to me talk about my fictional characters as if they're a part of my family, plotted with me, or been my cheerleader, I appreciate your continued support. Please know it hasn't gone unnoticed.

Last but certainly not least, to my four beautiful girls who have had to wait patiently when I said, "Just one more minute," when I obviously meant a lot more than one. I love that you get that I have deadlines and will sometimes keep me on task with your not-so-subtle reminders that "Mom… you should be working" during my designated times. I appreciate your support more than you'll ever know. Even though you can't read these books—because that might be *weird*—for both of us, I love that you keep asking. I love you all more than words can express. You're the reason I continue to strive and reach for my goals each day.

ALSO BY AMANDA SHELLEY

## Making The Call

**Dani**

As a bestselling romance author, most assume my life's glamorous, filled with combustible chemistry, and most of all, romance. Ha! I can only wish. With a deadline looming, I've escaped to my family's cabin on Anderson Island to free myself from distractions. My plan's great, until a man, who could pass as a cover model on one of my books, comes to my rescue. Is there chemistry? Sure. Is he everything I'd look for in a guy? Absolutely. But will my career be at risk if I give into my desire?

**Luke**

For a player, women line up outside the locker room. For coaches, we're lucky to get in the game. As the youngest NFL coach in the league, I live, eat, breathe, and even sleep football. To gear up for this season, I return to my home on Anderson Island for a much-needed break. When Dani literally crashes into my life, my mind's suddenly on the sexy brunette with a sailors mouth, rather than my team's next play. She has me dusting off another playbook entirely, making me wonder, did I make the right call?

https://geni.us/AmandaShelleyBooks

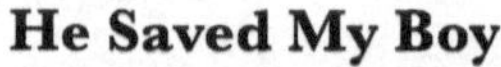

**He Saved My Boy**

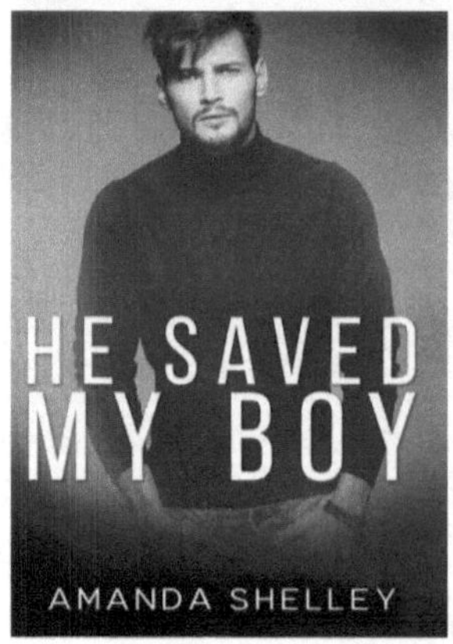



Davis is the first guy to catch my attention since... hell, I don't even know.

Instantly, he makes me think and feel things I've forgotten existed. It has been forever since I put my needs first, so I take the chance and let him light me up from the inside out.

Our night is the kind that will ruin me for all others.

But then I get the dreaded call.

I rush out without a second glance, knowing I'll likely never see him again.

My son will always come first—Always.

Imagine my surprise when Davis walks in, and I find he's the only one who can save my boy.

This cannot be happening—*I guess it's time to pull up my big girl panties and see what happens.*

https://geni.us/AmandaShelleyBooks

---

**Zander: A Perfectly Independent Series Novella**

Zander's known for being a player both on and off the court. When his name shows up as my next client, my heart stalls, and not in a good way. There's no way I'll survive the semester with him. I just don't have the patience.

However, when I need help, Zander makes a proposal I can't refuse.

He'll be my fake date to my best friend's wedding so I don't have to face my ex and his new girlfriend alone.

The weekend goes off without a hitch as we effortlessly pretend to have the time of our lives.

All is perfect… until I realize my feelings for Zander are no longer an act.

What will I do when our arrangement comes to an end?

https://geni.us/AmandaShelleyBooks

---

**Drew: Book One of the Perfectly Independent Series**

### *Of all people, why him?*

He didn't EVEN bother introducing himself, just assumed I knew him from his fame on the court.

I nearly died on the spot when our professor announced we were permanent lab partners. Between his arrogance and the constant interruption from basketball groupies, there's no way I'll survive this semester.

Sure, he's hotter than anyone I've ever seen in a science lab with his sexy blue eyes, cute dimple, and muscles for days - but I can't afford *his* kind of distractions.

Okay. Deep breath.

I can do this.

After all, it's only one semester.

Just when I think my self-control is in check, he does something to show me that he isn't the egotistical, self-centered jerk I thought he was.

How can his stupid smile suddenly make my mind melt, heart race, and palms sweat?

***If I take this chance on Drew, will my perfectly laid out plans disappear?***

https://geni.us/AmandaShelleyBooks

---

**Vince: Book Two of the Perfectly Independent Series**

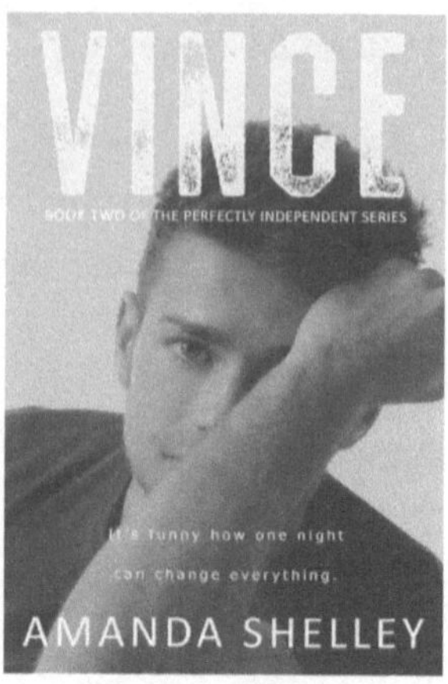


**It's funny how one night can change everything.**

As a bartender near campus, I'm certain I've heard it all. Rarely a shift passes without some guy taking his best shot, hoping I'll end my self-proclaimed dating diet.

Of course, this is exactly how I meet Vince.

Except, he isn't the one running his mouth.

No, he simply shuts down his idiotic friend, then stops my heart with the simplest of smiles and walks away.

Just when I force myself to forget him, he bumps into me on campus.

Our connection is consuming, and my world is knocked off kilter. It's far beyond physical attraction. He's smart, sexy, and feels like—home?

*Wait, that can't be right...*

Whatever it is, Vince has me breaking my rules to spend time with him.

My entire life I've prepared for meeting the wrong guys.

*What the hell should I do when I find the right one?*

https://geni.us/AmandaShelleyBooks

## Damien: Book Three of the Perfectly Independent Series

Beautiful girls are not hard to find at Columbia River University.

The coeds on campus are great to look at but I was over that scene after graduation three years ago.

These days, outside of being part of the largest civil engineering job on campus, all I'm searching for is a decent meal and some peace and quiet. It's why I'm happy to have found what I consider a hidden gem in the diner I frequent.

All I need to do is finish this job and move on to the next by year's end.

Should be easy enough. Only when Vanessa walks up with a sexy smile and a mouth full of sass, she does more than take my order. She completely takes my breath away.

Next thing I know, I'm here every morning, making every excuse to dine with this intriguing woman. Not only is she smart and sexy, but she's laser focused on reaching the goals she's set for herself.

The more I get to know her, the more I'm convinced she's the one. I just have to find a way to get her to deviate from her perfectly laid plans and take a chance on me.

https://geni.us/AmandaShelleyBooks

**The Summer Dare**

**Leave it to Nana to think of everything.**

After a grueling semester, I'm ready for a peaceful summer in Seaside with my sisters.

Imagine my surprise, when I'm woken by the screeching sound of a saw coming through my wall, the first official morning of break.

Not only did I come flying out of bed swinging, but I gave Ryan, the unsuspecting carpenter the surprise of his life, when I came wielding my killer coat hanger and all.

Too bad, I was only in a tank and undies and it wasn't nearly as effective as I'd hoped.

Of course, he insists he's only doing his job. Since it's Nana's last request to care for us, I can't refuse.

However, I won't let a tall, pesky, sexy as sin, know-it-all get in my way of my summer plans. I pretend I ignore him – that is until my youngest sister pokes her nose in my business and throws down a dare I can't back down from.

Kiss the next single guy who walks up to the bonfire – or explain to my sisters why I get riled up over the contractor.

When Ryan suddenly appears, I know I'm screwed in more ways than one.

Not only will my sisters learn my secret, but from the determined look on Ryan's face, I'm afraid he's eager to reveal it to the world as well.

What have I gotten myself into?

*As I walk toward him, one thing is certain – this summer dare will either make or break me.*

https://geni.us/AmandaShelleyBooks

---

**The Summer Ultimatum**

Watching my sister fall in love last summer gave me something I hadn't expected—hope. It gave me hope that there might be someone out there for me and hope that I might get past my misguided fears and finally let someone in.

With my help, Ryan's planning the most epic proposal. I just have to get the know-it-all musician I work with to fall in line to make it work.

Jax is wicked smart, extremely talented, and sexy as sin. But he can't see the forest for the trees when it comes to his potential. He'd rather keep playing in dive bars along the coast than take a real shot at success.

When the Seaside festival has a music competition, I present Jax with an ultimatum that will either make or break both our careers.

I've laid it all on the line, but can he?

https://geni.us/AmandaShelleyBooks

**The Summer Proposal**

My sisters are dropping like flies.

They're falling in love and having the time of their lives.

Don't get me wrong, I'm ecstatic for them. I love seeing them happy.

But I'm not ready for that type of commitment.

I can't even keep a plant alive, let alone find someone worthy of getting past a third date.

As the only sister done with school and single as a pringle, I have to do something fast, or I'll be my matchmaking aunt's next victim.

When Jax's drummer joins him for the summer and needs some help with his image, I make him a deal he can't refuse.

All is perfect—until I realize my summer proposal has one minor flaw.

Our relationship may be a sham, but there's nothing fake about my feelings for Finn.

https://geni.us/AmandaShelleyBooks

## The Summer Arrangement

One, two, three—it's all down to me.

As the youngest and only single Lancaster, I'm eager to spend my summer in Seaside, Oregon, with my sisters. It's something I've looked forward to all year, and I'm determined to make every minute count. After all, I've only got one year before I graduate from college and have to adult for real.

However, if I want to graduate debt free, I need to work. I have a lead on the perfect summer job with the nanny agency I've spent the last three summers catering to.

I just have to win over an adorable three-year-old and convince her single dad I'm the right one for the job.

Simple enough, right?

Except when I show up at his door, I'm shocked to find he's the guy I hooked up with a few times last semester.

This cannot be happening.

I need this job. There's too much on the line to walk away. Maybe we can put the past behind us and make some sort of summer arrangement?

https://geni.us/AmandaShelleyBooks

---

**The Summer I Found Home**

Being a pilot is all I've ever known.

I served my country and I'm damn proud of my career.

But sacrifices were made, especially when it came to family.

I've missed first steps, first days of school, and first dates to name a few.

My kids grew up. They're having families of their own.

Was it worth it?

When an opportunity brings me to Seaside, I jump feet first no questions asked.

It means experiencing all those firsts with my grandkids.

With family as my focus and my guard down, I don't even see Faye coming.

She's a force to be reckoned with and has me holding on for dear life.

I thought our ship had sailed, but now that I'm home for good—I just might get more than one second chance.

arrangement?

https://geni.us/AmandaShelleyBooks

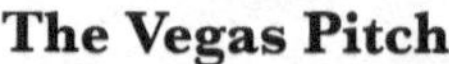

**The Vegas Pitch**

This pitch could make or break my career.

Not only will it set a personal record for the biggest account I've ever landed, but it could set my newfound company three years ahead of schedule for expansion.

Thank god I've got Nate Bellinger on my team.

Even though I had my reservations hiring the sexiest man I've ever laid eyes on – he more than meets my expectations with his hard work and determination. Together, we've formed a solid team and play off each other perfectly.

As we wait for the final verdict, I begrudgingly take Nate up on his offer for a night on the town. After all, this is Vegas and I need to let the chips fall where they may.

Imagine my surprise when I wake up the next morning to find we've not only won the campaign, but I'm apparently married to the man I've only ever let myself fantasize about.

The kicker of it all – he has no intentions of letting me go.

But what will it mean once we leave Vegas?

https://geni.us/AmandaShelleyBooks

**Resilience: Book One of Resilience Duet**

**Resolution: Book Two of Resilience Duet**

Samantha never saw Enzo coming.

As the dust settles from her divorce, her life is full. She doesn't have time for distractions. She's too busy running her own company and checking off numerous items from her kids' demanding schedule to have a life of her own.

Then he walks into her kitchen with his breathtaking green eyes and a mischievous grin. He's there to surprise his father - her contractor, but his presence makes everything off kilter.

Enzo's perfectly content with his adventurous life as an elite rescue pilot, until a harmless prank turns on him. Instead of surprising his father, he finds his world thrown off course by the beautiful woman with a sexy smile, wicked sass and the mouthwatering ability to keep him on his toes.

With his limited time on leave, is she worth the risk to his heart?

https://geni.us/AmandaShelleyBooks

**Collide: A Sweet Romance**

Falling head over heels was the last thing I expected.

Literally.

Coffee is everywhere – and more than my ego is bruised.

When the handsome stranger I plowed into calls me by name, mortification sinks in.

He rushes off to class. I run home to change, hoping to forget the whole incident.

If only I could be so lucky.

I quickly find it's a small world and Gavin Wallace is completely unavoidable. Everywhere I turn he's there. In my classes. Hanging with my friends.

I've got his full attention and I have to admit, I like it a lot more than I should.

https://geni.us/AmandaShelleyBooks